Mistletoe Love Match

A Love Match Legacy Holiday Novella

Krista Sandor

Candy Castle Books

Chapter One

Calliope Cress

Calliope Cress was on the cusp of sweet release.

Crammed into a snug broom closet, she gripped the lip of a shelf piled high with rolls of toilet paper and hummed her pleasure. "That feels so bloody good," she bit out in a breathy British accent, then immediately wanted to take it back—not because she was upset about teetering on the brink of orgasmic bliss. If anyone needed a trip to O-town, it was her.

It was Christmas Eve, and she'd gotten roped into volunteering in the Helping Hands Community Center's childcare room for the final day of a health and wellness fair. She'd been there for the last seven and a half hours looking after the medical staff's children. Twenty kids in one place with every child amped up on dreams of what they'd find under the Christmas tree had been like herding cats. But as crazy as it was in the classroom, that wasn't what had her prickly with irritation and wound as tight as a spring on the verge of snapping.

The problem was the infuriating man on his knees in front of her going to town like he was a horny old Saint Nick and she was a plate of freshly baked Christmas cookies.

The wanker with a magic mouth, Alec Lamb.

1

A man she couldn't escape.

And why couldn't she avoid him?

He was volunteering at the community center, too. Thank God he wasn't stationed in the classroom. He was a doctor in training—a medical school student—and was on the other side of the building, tending to patients.

Oh, and they resided in the same bloody house.

That's right. The. Same. House.

Her brother's house.

Well, it wasn't just her brother's home.

Alec's older sister, Libby, was engaged to Calliope's older brother, Erasmus—or Raz, as he was known to his close friends and family. They lived together with Raz's son, Sebastian. Libby, Raz, and the lad made a darling trio. Calliope adored her nephew, and she loved her soon-to-be sister-in-law. The chick was a yoga sensation and a shrewd businesswoman. But Libby had one glaring fault—well, two, to be exact—Alec Lamb and his twin brother, Anders, men who happened to be the same age as her and her twin sister, Callista.

Yes, twins.

It was a nauseating double twin-a-palooza situation. And it had been like that for the last four months.

Alec and Anders were supposed to attend medical school in a study-abroad program in Ecuador, but they'd decided to complete their first semester in Denver to be with their sister. She and Callista had left their home in London to teach in South Korea. Instead of returning to their posh flat in Chelsea after their teaching stint ended, they'd traveled to Colorado to spend time with Raz, Libby, and Sebastian.

Little did she know she'd be stuck in the wonder-twins four-some from hell.

And that statement demanded a point of bloody clari-fication.

It wasn't hell being with her sister. They'd been inseparable their entire lives. And even Anders, with his easy smile and stupid jokes, was tolerable. What made it a living hell was that Callista and Anders had clicked from the minute they'd locked eyes. It was like something out of one of those American Hallmark movies, with the two lovebirds blushing like schoolchildren and fawning all over each other.

Anders, how sweet of you to find a shop that carries my favorite English toffees.

Callista, I love this stethoscope. It's such a thoughtful gift.

Gag City.

She'd had a decidedly different reaction to Alec.

Despite having her leg slung over his shoulder and her panties hanging off her ankle as he worked her with his mouth, she despised the man. The bloke was aloof and as rigid as an ironing board. The stick shoved up the man's arse was in there tighter than Excalibur stuck in stone.

And she couldn't get away from him. The rhythm of her life went like this: Alec was always with Anders. Anders was always with Callista, which meant she had to tag along—for her sister's sake, of course.

It was one thing to entertain a little crush, but she wasn't about to let Callista fall hard and fast for Anders Lamb. She knew her sister as well as she knew herself. Callista wasn't ready for a serious relationship. They were twenty-two years old. They'd graduated with degrees in elementary education and had plans to teach abroad and see the world. Not to mention, Alec and Anders would return to Ecuador soon to continue their studies. But that didn't matter to Callista. Anders Lamb was the only thing her sister seemed to be able to focus on these days. And that's why Calliope had to pull a Jane Austen and act like the modern-day Victorian cockblock.

Unfortunately, she had to do this with Alec sneering at her like Ebenezer Scrooge.

She'd wake up, ready to spend the day with her sister, and hello, moody wanker. Alec was always in the background, watching her from every angle. Even when everyone in the house was fast asleep, she couldn't avoid the man.

She'd pop downstairs for a midnight snack, and brooding Alec would be there, guzzling a glass of milk or noshing on an apple, which was utter insanity. Who in their right mind snacked on apples in the middle of the night?

If up at a ridiculous hour when most normal people were fast asleep, the only decent thing to do was to stand in front of the fridge with the doors wide open and gorge on the most delicious, calorie-laden food available. Anyone who drank skim milk and chomped on an apple like a mule at two a.m. had to be a bloody psychopath.

But he was a gorgeous psychopath.

Damn the man for sauntering into the kitchen in nothing but gray sweatpants—gray sweatpants that had given her a glimpse of the man's equipment below the waistband. On a scale of one to ten, Alec Lamb was a solid negative three thousand in personality, but his cock was off the bloody charts. Honestly, it wasn't her fault for jumping the guy like she'd majored in pole vaulting at uni. What woman could resist a man in gray sweatpants? It had to be programmed into female DNA. She'd spy the stupid, sexy bloke and instantly become wet and go weak in the knees at the sight of the loungewear hugging the man in all the right places.

But there was more.

Above his giant cock, the man rocked washboard abs. Sweatpants plus a ripped physique and the aloof set of his jaw had her itching to claw his eyes out, which morphed into clawing her fingernails down his back.

He barely uttered a word to her when they were in the company of Callista and Anders. But the lines between lust and loathing blurred when the house was still and it was just the two of them.

Had she wanted to shag his brains out in the pantry next to a box of corn flakes and fifty billion canisters of quinoa nearly every night since they'd arrived in Denver?

Hell to the no!

Okay, *hell to the no* might be a bit of an exaggeration.

The sex was toe-curlingly explosive. The man knew what he was doing in the getting down and dirty department. But it was only sex—nothing more. It was a reaction to a fit bloke in gray sweatpants. It could happen to anyone. The truth was, it had been one hell of a hot minute since she'd had a proper shag. Between not getting any in ages and the tension building between herself and Alec, she'd been on the brink of detonating. And the stone-faced shell of a man appeared to feel the same way.

It only made sense to start banging away to release the pent-up frustration.

Right or wrong, that's how they'd carried on since she'd arrived at her brother's place in Denver's ritzy Crystal Hills neighborhood—August, September, October, November, and for the better part of December.

Still, something about today was different.

Callista and Anders, along with their friends and families, had left Denver a few days ago. They'd headed southwest to spend the Christmas holiday in the mountain town of Rickety Rock, Colorado. Her brother and Libby owned a sprawling Victorian vacation home, and her granny Fin resided in the guesthouse.

Calliope should have been there, directing her sister's attention away from Anders. But thanks to the universe behaving like a knob-headed plonker, she and Alec had to stay behind to work at the health fair. She couldn't say no. Her brother and Libby were huge supporters of the Helping Hands Community Center. Not to mention, she wanted to volunteer. She was a teacher—and a damned good one. Nobody went into education for the money. She did it because she genuinely loved teaching and wanted to give back. Helping Hands was just the sort of place she wanted to end up once she and Callista had traveled the world.

Still, if she'd had a crystal ball years ago and been able to see that her passion for education would land her in the same building as the exasperating Alec Lamb, she would have gone into accounting or underwater basket weaving—anything to put space between herself and the med school wanker.

At least she didn't have to drive to Rickety Rock with the man. Her brother had set her up with a smart little Mini Cooper. She could blast the music and get Alec out of her head, but first, she needed Doctor Booty Call to get her off—to help her relax. It was nothing more than that. This would be the last time she'd have it off with him. They couldn't carry on like this in Rickety Rock. There'd be too many people at Raz's mountain home and a slew of kids to boot. Knocking out a quickie in the pantry couldn't happen with four families under one roof.

Alec tightened his hold on her arse and pressed a kiss to her inner thigh. "How good is it, Calliope?" he rasped in his stupid, sexy voice.

Bloody idiot.

She met the man's searing amber gaze. "You know it's good, or I wouldn't have said it."

A cocky smirk twisted the man's lips—lips that should have been pressed between her thighs. "How good?" he demanded, then grazed his teeth across her sensitive skin.

She gasped as a cascade of tingles tittered through her core.

Dammit, she loved it when he did that. She tangled her fingers in his jet-black hair and formulated a reply. "It's perfectly adequate."

"Adequate?" he repeated, his cocksure smirk widening into a sly grin. But before she could put together a pithy reply, he returned to working her like his mouth had a vibration mode.

"That's it," she moaned when the bloke paused, teasing her like the wanker he was.

"You pulled me into this closet, Calliope Cress. I doubt you would have done that for perfectly adequate oral sex."

Who actually called it oral sex?

"I've only got a fifteen-minute break. What did you want me to do? Book a room at the Waldorf Astoria?" she shot back.

Alec hummed a smug little laugh. "They don't have a Waldorf Astoria in Denver."

This tosser!

She gathered herself as much as a woman could with a man's head buried between her thighs. "You know what I mean. And you pulled me into the laundry room last night."

"I had laundry to do," he answered, massaging her with the pads of his fingers as he drank her in. And God help her, she had to bite her lip to keep from purring like a cat.

She rocked her hips, unable to stop herself from riding his hand. "No, you had *me* to do, Dr. Wanker."

Ugh! She'd uttered another thing she couldn't take back.

Alec hummed his amusement, and the vibration set her body aflame.

This psychopath liked it when she called him Dr. Wanker. But she couldn't help herself. The man scrambled her brain.

She twisted her fingers in his hair and tensed. She was close —so bloody close. "Fine, it feels amazing, but you're still a right daft sod, Alec Lamb," she got out, her East London accent growing more pronounced as she inched closer to sweet release.

He set his mouth to super-duper oral sex mode and oral-sexed the hell out of her.

She released a breathy moan, then made the mistake of looking down.

She caught Alec's eye. He was watching her as he worked her. She inhaled a sharp breath. This erotic act triggered a delicious rush of heat. It swept through her in a titillating whoosh. There was no denying it. She liked having his eyes trained on her.

Mischief flickered in his gaze, and he dialed up the pressure.

Every sensation amplified. Pleasure thrummed, matching the rapid beat of her heart.

Her orgasm tore through her, and she couldn't look away. The heat pulsing through her body ignited like a wildfire fueled by ravenous desire. She pressed her palm to her lips to stifle her dirty-girl moans.

And that's when it happened.

In these tender moments, when she couldn't get any more vulnerable, another side—a secret side—of Alec Lamb emerged. The judgmental stick in the mud disappeared. His eyes glittered with drunken awe as he claimed her with his mouth. It was almost as if he wasn't a complete bloody wanker. He was a man driven by passion—passion for making her come like the world was about to end, and this was the last chance he'd get to taste her.

Her chest heaved as she floated down from orgasmic bliss and back to reality. Reduced to a noodle, she exhaled a sated sigh as Alec shifted beneath her. He gently removed her leg from his shoulder. But once her foot hit the floor, he didn't stop touching her, and she didn't immediately reach for her knickers.

She liked what came next too much.

He trailed his hands up the sides of her body as he rose to his full height and towered over her. She'd never admit it, but it comforted her to be close to him. She rested her head against his chest and caught her breath as he gathered her into his embrace.

"Was that adequate enough for you?" he asked. And bloody hell, that voice. She could hear the self-satisfied lilt to his question, and her treacherous core clenched. Her body ached, ready for round two with this man.

Stop!

They couldn't go on like this. She had to focus on the future and make sure Callista didn't fall for Anders.

She broke free and scowled at the beautiful wanker. "It'll do because we're done."

He glanced at his watch. "We have six minutes. You, of all people, know what I can do in that amount of time."

Her core clenched. Oh yeah, she knew. But she had to be strong. "We can't do this anymore, Alec. It's been fun, but we've exhausted this passing flirtation."

A muscle ticked in his jaw, and his sparkling gaze hardened into a curmudgeon glare. "Okay," he answered with an aloof shrug.

Okay?

She'd expected a bit more of a reaction than a blasé *okay*. Didn't he at least want to ask her why she'd decided to put the kibosh on their secret tryst? Was it that easy for the man to turn off his emotions?

Gah! She growled her irritation. She had to get out of there, finish her shift, and join her sister. She parted her lips, prepared to tell Dr. Wanker to piss off, when the click of footsteps and a pair of voices left her speechless.

"Ho, ho, ho, have you seen Alec Lamb?" a man asked in an overdone Santa voice.

"One of the volunteers said they saw him walking down this hallway with Calliope Cress, Mr. Claus," a woman answered.

"She's on her break, and I was hoping to have a word with her. We can look for them together."

Oh no!

Calliope's jaw dropped, and the prickle of impending doom spider-crawled down her spine.

She recognized the voices.

What were they supposed to do?

She held her breath and met Alec's gaze. He'd turned the color of dirty dishwater. He was thinking the same thing she was. They were seconds away from landing themselves on the naughty list.

Chapter Two

Alec Lamb

T he clap of footsteps stopped, and Alec froze.
Christ, how he wished it was the real Saint Nick
and Mrs. Claus.

But it wasn't.

It was Louise and Ralph Dagby—the husband-and-wife
team who ran the Helping Hands community center. The pair
had paused outside the supply closet door.

He and Calliope were trapped.

This was bad.

No, this was a catastrophe. They couldn't get caught looking
like a pair of depraved holiday hooligans. He wasn't the type of
doctor-in-training who got it on in a supply closet.

Shit—that statement wasn't accurate, was it?

He'd just gotten it on in a supply closet, but it wasn't like
him to behave like a sex-crazed maniac. The maddeningly beautiful Calliope Cress was to blame for that. To be fair, he wasn't
neglecting his duties. Thanks to some winter weather rolling in,
the health fair traffic had slowed in the last hour. That was the
only reason he'd taken a break. And he never took breaks.
However, had he strolled toward the other side of the building

on purpose because he knew Calliope was volunteering in the childcare room?

No, of course not.

He'd been cooped up in a makeshift cubicle checking vitals for the last seven and a half hours. He was merely stretching his legs, which meant walking the length of a hallway that just happened to go by the childcare area.

Had he passed by her classroom window four times? All right, five times—possibly six?

Yes, he had.

And when he'd heard the lead teacher tell Calliope she could take a fifteen-minute break, had his pulse shot up like he was about to go into cardiac arrest and had his blood supply headed south, leaving him in a state of disorientation known acutely as *Calliope-itis*?

Maybe.

Fine . . . yes.

From the moment she'd scowled at him four months ago and called him Dr. Wanker, he'd lost all perspective regarding his sister's fiancé's little sister.

Sweet Jesus, say that five times fast.

"Alec," Calliope mouthed. Urgency flashed in her gray eyes as she pointed at the door.

Dammit! They had company. "I know," he mouthed back.

She raised her hands and busted out the international expression for what-the-hell-should-we-do?

Think, think, think.

"Since we're here," Louise remarked, "let me grab a few rolls of toilet paper. I noticed the restrooms near the entrance were running low."

Shit! There was nowhere to hide, and he couldn't allow the Dagbys to find them like this. Louise and Ralph were friends with his sister and her fiancé, Erasmus Cress. If the community center directors caught them in a broom closet, they'd surely mention it to Libby or Raz. And while Raz was a great guy, Calliope's brother was also the world's heavyweight boxing champion. He sure as hell didn't want to get on the wrong side of a man who could knock a dude out with one punch.

Not to mention, he had enough to worry about these days.

His brother seemed to be attached at the hip to Calliope's sister. Callista Cress was a perfectly lovely human being, but he and Anders didn't have time for distractions. They had to focus on their studies. And they certainly couldn't entertain a serious romantic relationships. They had to return to Ecuador. They'd completed their first semester of med school in Colorado, and he'd loved spending time with Libby, but a plan was a plan. They'd agreed to study abroad, and he couldn't let his brother get sidetracked.

"Alec!" Calliope whispered-screamed, then whipped his stethoscope off the shelf and used it to smack him in the chest.

"Ow!" he whisper-yelled back, taking the medical instrument from her and resting it around his neck. He should educate her on how to properly handle his equipment, but there was no time for a lecture—or even a stern rebuke. He had to act. He straightened his stethoscope, scanned the snug space, and spied salvation.

Toilet paper to the rescue.

He swiped two rolls off the shelf and handed one to Calliope. "Follow my lead," he hissed, not exactly sure what that would look like, but as a doctor, he'd need to think quickly and make snap decisions.

He swung open the door and burst into the hallway. "See, Calliope, this is where they store the toilet paper. Anytime you require an extra roll, you can find it here," he announced like a deranged tour guide. He glanced over his shoulder and met Calliope's gaze.

She cringed, then patted her lips. Why the hell would she do that?

Dammit, he didn't have time to ponder her bizarre reaction. He had to address the Louise and Ralph situation. "Hello, Mr. and Mrs. Dagby, aren't you looking festive." Somewhere between greeting him this morning and now, the Dagbys had changed into Mr. and Mrs. Claus costumes.

"We do it for the kids every year," Ralph said, glancing into the supply closet, then sharing a curious look with Louise.

"You're probably wondering how we ended up inside the closet with the door closed," Calliope blurted.

Oh shit!

"And there's a very good and very reasonable explanation," she continued.

All he could do was pray she actually had a reason.

"And that is?" Ralph asked with a perplexed bend to the question.

She cleared her throat and lifted her chin. "An immersive experience—in the supply closet."

"An immersive experience?" Louise repeated with a crinkle to her brow.

"Absolutely," Calliope beamed. "As a teacher, I need to be prepared, which means identifying the closest location to procure items for the loo. It's important to ingrain the closet into my memory because children go to the bathroom and require toilet paper. It's . . . biological," she finished, then threw him a glance that said *help a woman out.*

She'd rattled off one hell of a word salad, but he could work with biology.

He nodded vigorously, channeling a bobblehead doll. "As someone training to become a doctor, I agree with that statement. Children do, in fact, use the restroom. It's a biological bodily function."

Now they sounded insane.

"And speaking of children," Calliope said, jumping in, "they enjoyed it when you stopped by the classroom." She blessedly steered the conversation away from excretion and freaking toilet paper. Her posture relaxed for a second until she glanced down. She inhaled a sharp breath, then went as stiff as a board before turning almost as white as Ralph's fake Santa beard.

What had gotten into her?

As far as he could tell, they were in the clear.

Then he looked down too, and what he saw encasing Calliope's ankle damn near had his heart beating itself out of his chest like he was experiencing the most severe case of tachycardia known to mankind. He blinked, but the image remained the same. And what had his heart ready to explode?

A pair of emerald-green silk panties that just happened to be haphazardly looped around her booted foot.

It was weird enough that they'd emerged from the broom closet. Their bullshit toilet paper explanation was a flimsy excuse at best. How were they supposed to explain the location of her underwear?

Louise Dagby eyed him closely, which was a good thing. He had to keep the couple from looking down.

"I see someone enjoyed the doughnuts Cupid Bakery donated," the woman commented.

Doughnuts?

What was she talking about?

He frowned. "I don't eat doughnuts, Mrs. Dagby. I only eat clean—apples, quinoa, kale—"

"—and doughnuts. You made an exception because it's Christmas Eve," Calliope chimed as she tore off a sheet of toilet paper and wiped his mouth like he was a toddler who'd just smashed his face into a bowl of spaghetti.

And then it hit him. He wasn't covered in doughnut glaze. He had Calliope on his lips.

"You had four doughnuts, right, Alec? That's why your lips are so shiny," she continued with a devilish smirk. "You crammed them into your mouth like you'd never tasted anything so delicious in your entire life."

Now she was messing with him.

But two could play that game.

"The doughnuts were delicious. I'll give you that. I'm not sure I'd call them the best I've ever had. They were . . . adequate."

Boom!

That wiped the sexy little smirk off her face.

Was he lying?

Yeah, he was. He fucking loved how she tasted, but Alec sure as hell couldn't let her know that.

"Adequate?" Calliope repeated. She shifted her stance, and the movement swished her panties against the floor. He'd forgotten they had decorative gold rings on each side. The bits of metal scraped the ceramic tiles, and the damned cocoon of a hallway amplified the sound.

Panic jolted through him, and terror flashed in Calliope's eyes. Before either could utter a reply, Louise's gaze dropped to the ground.

"What's that green fabric around your ankle, Calliope?"

Dammit!

He'd been so preoccupied going toe-to-toe with the maddeningly beautiful pantyless woman that he'd forgotten about running interference on the underwear situation.

Louise and Ralph stared at the emerald G-string.

"Is that a pair of underwear?" Louise pressed.

"Oh, those," Calliope eked out like it was commonplace for one's undergarments to spontaneously appear at one's feet.

"They must have fallen out of my . . . pocket. Yes, my pocket. They're a Christmas present for . . ." She trailed off, but he had a brilliant idea and was right there to save the day.

"They're for your granny Finola. You got your granny non-granny panties for Christmas—in a festive color, no less," he supplied, and dammit, the whole granny-panty response had sounded a lot better in his head. But there was no going back now.

Calliope plastered on a grin that would put a beauty queen to shame. "Yep, sexy Christmas-tree-colored knickers for my granny. My granny loves 'em," she added, then in a perplexing cheerleader-like movement, she kicked her panty leg. The underwear sailed through the air. They soared in a graceful arc and landed on . . . his face.

This could not get any worse.

He peeled the silk from his cheek and handed them to his partner in supply-closet crime. "You should have them gift-wrapped or find a festive bag and dress it up with a bow."

Find a festive bag and dress it up with a bow?

Was he having an aneurysm?

He shifted his stance and noticed something strange—well, not quite as bizarre as having a pair of panties fly through the air and smack you in the face, but odd, nonetheless. "It's awfully quiet in here," he remarked.

"I don't hear anything coming from the classrooms," Calliope noted. "Are you closing early?"

"We are," Ralph answered. "The snow has picked up, and we wanted our staff and volunteers to get home safely before the roads got too icy. Most everyone has cleared out. We just have to sign off on a delivery that should be here any minute, then we're heading over to my sister's house to celebrate Christmas Eve."

"It's a good thing we ran into you. We needed to speak with you both before you left," Louise added.

17

Calliope stuffed the panties into the pocket of her skirt. "Is something wrong?"

Ralph and Louise shared another curious look.

Were their gooses cooked? Had the pair figured out what they were doing in that closet?

"Actually, something might be very right," Ralph offered up.

Maybe their luck was changing.

"Alec, dear?" Louise said, watching him closely.

Shit! Did he still have Calliope on his face?

"Yes?" he answered, then fake coughed into his elbow and rubbed his chin on the sleeve of his scrubs. It wasn't the smoothest of moves. Calliope pressing her lips into a hard line to keep from laughing clued him in on that. But what was he supposed to do? Ask for Calliope to give him another once-over with a wad of toilet paper?

"Have you decided if you're going to stay in Colorado, like your brother? We're excited he'll be able to continue volunteering here," Louise dropped like a bomb.

What the fuck?

He'd like to think that Louise was wrong, but the woman was as sharp as a tack. She wouldn't mix up something like that, would she?

"Nothing is definitive," he answered, going for the vaguest response possible. He had to get ahold of Anders to find out what the hell the man had told Louise Dagby—that he hadn't shared with him.

He and Anders didn't keep anything from each other.

Scratch that. He'd kept his Calliope situation from his brother.

Maybe they did have secrets.

"And Callista asked if I'd be a reference for her," Ralph added, addressing Calliope.

"For what?" his pantyless partner pressed.

"She's looking into open teaching positions in the area. I'd be happy to write a recommendation for you as well. We've been so lucky to have such gifted teachers volunteering in our childcare rooms."

Now it was Calliope's turn to look like the Dagbys had just hurled a Frosty-the-Snowman-sized snowball at her face.

"Callista wants to teach in Denver?" she repeated.

This was news to him—and clearly to her, too.

Holy shit! Could Anders and Callista have their own secret that went beyond making googly eyes at each other?

"It would be such a gift to have you all here, wouldn't it, Louise?" Ralph continued. "We're so fond of Libby and Erasmus and, of course, Sebastian, too. I'm sure they'd be delighted to have you close by as well."

Calliope parted her lips, but nothing came out.

At least he wasn't the only one who'd gotten bamboozled by Kringle lookalikes.

"No, don't tell us now," Ralph said excitedly and waved them off. "Louise and I will text you tomorrow. Your answer can be a Christmas surprise," he finished, then added a hearty *ho, ho, ho*.

"And we'll take those off your hands," Louise said, relieving them of their toilet paper. The woman glanced at the ceiling. "And now you've got to kiss."

Kiss?

He was still reeling from the Anders and Callista revelations—and now these people wanted him to kiss Calliope? Was there some Christmas delirium going around that made everyone lose their minds? He shared a perplexed look with his supply closet companion.

"We have to kiss because we gave you the toilet paper?" Calliope asked.

Louise chuckled. "No, you have to kiss because you're standing beneath the mistletoe."

Alec looked up, and the woman wasn't wrong. A green sprig with red berries hung from above.

Ralph nodded. "It's a Christmas tradition. It would be bad luck if you didn't."

"I didn't notice it before," Calliope said, staring up at the petite spray of green leaves tied with a white ribbon.

"Neither did I," added Alec, studying the tiny red berries and pointy leaves. Who the hell would hang mistletoe in front of a supply closet?

"A kiss under the mistletoe can change everything," Louise offered. "It can lead you in a direction you never expected."

What the hell did that mean?

He smiled politely, but he didn't want anything to change. He met Calliope's eye. They appeared to agree on that point. She looked ready to yank the mistletoe from the ceiling and stomp it into bits.

"Ralph, Louise," a voice echoed from the end of the hall. "The truck's here. They need you to sign off on the delivery before you leave."

Saved by the delivery truck. Alec breathed a sigh of relief.

"Merry Christmas, you two," Louise said and patted his arm.

"Until tomorrow," Ralph remarked over his shoulder as the pair headed down the hallway. "And don't forget to get in a kiss. The mistletoe doesn't forget."

The Dagbys had barely turned the corner when Calliope huffed and turned on her heel. "I don't care if it's a Christmas tradition. I'm not kissing you under any bloody mistletoe, Dr. Wanker," she muttered as she threw the scrap of toilet paper in a trash can, then tore down the hallway.

"Are you mad at me?" He had to break into a jog to keep up.

"Yeah, I'm mad at you," she hissed, then charged into the darkened childcare room and grabbed her purse and coat.

"Why?"

"Why?" she shot back. "Because your bloody brother is corrupting my sister."

"You think my brother is to blame?" he threw back, following a step behind her as she headed for the exit. He grabbed his jacket off the rack near the door. He barely had one arm in the coat sleeve when Calliope bolted out of the center and into the snowstorm.

"Yeah, he's to blame," she snarled, shivering as she strutted through the parking lot, pantyless in boots and a skirt that hit mid-thigh. Aside from prancing around in a bikini, Calliope's current outfit might just have been the worst clothing choice for this kind of weather.

He squinted and blinked the blowing snow from his eyes. It had really picked up, and it was freaking freezing. "Slow down, Calliope! It could be icy, and you need to take my coat."

"You want me to take your coat?"

"I'd prefer not to treat you for hypothermia or frostbite. So yeah, at least tie it around your bare legs."

She whipped around and poked him in the chest as snowflakes accumulated on her eyelashes and in her honey-brown hair. She looked like a beautifully irate snow princess. "I'm fine, Dr. Wanker." She scoffed. "Why are you so cool and collected? Aren't you furious about Callista and Anders?"

He was furious, but he didn't show it by plowing through an icy parking lot.

She rifled through her purse, pulled out a set of keys, and hit a button on the fob, but nothing chirped. "Bloody stupid car," she muttered, then unlocked her Mini Cooper manually. She threw her purse on the passenger side, settled herself into the driver's seat, then glared at him. "Louise and Ralph must be confused. There's no way Callista would make plans to stay in Denver with Anders. Maybe the Dagbys are already trollied. It is the holidays."

"Trollied?" he repeated.

"It means drunk," she cried and banged her palms on the steering wheel.

He shook his head. "They didn't appear intoxicated. I didn't observe any lack of balance, and their speech wasn't slurred. I also didn't smell alcohol on their breath. When a person is intoxicated—"

"I don't want your clinical opinion, Dr. Wanker," she interrupted. "What they were saying about Callista has to be complete bullocks." She pulled her cell phone from her bag, then shrieked.

He'd never seen her like this before. "Do you need medical attention?"

"I need a mobile that isn't at one percent. I've got to talk to my sister. I'll just charge it while I drive."

"Are you sure you should be driving?" he asked as she pushed the button to start the car. But just like when she'd tried to unlock it with the fob, nothing happened.

"No, no, no," she lamented. "Just bloody work."

He shielded his eyes from the snow. This storm would only intensify, and there was only one option. "We're both going to Rickety Rock. You can ride with me. It'll be dark soon. We need to get on the road."

She pounded the steering wheel again and emitted a piercing yelp.

This tantrum wasn't helping.

He glanced at the darkening clouds. This storm was nowhere near over, and they didn't have time for screaming and abusing car parts in a parking lot. "Do you want to come with me, or do you want to keep assaulting the steering wheel until you succumb to hypothermia or break your wrists? My car's right there, for Christ's sake," he added and pointed toward his Jeep.

She banged the steering wheel again. This woman made him wish he were trollied.

"Calliope, I'm offering you a ride. Take it or leave it."

She rested her head on the steering wheel. "I'll take it. But I'm not happy about it."

No shit.

He sighed. "Where's your bag?"

"In the back," she answered, then reached behind the seat and manually unlocked the back door.

He retrieved her suitcase and caught sight of the luggage tag. It was a custom plastic label with a photo of Calliope and Callista making kissy lips. He smiled at the image. He couldn't help it. If anyone could understand the connection between twins, it was her.

"Maybe you're right," he began gently. "The Dagbys might have misconstrued the situation with our siblings. Callista and Anders could have asked about opportunities in Denver . . . for the future," he said, offering her his hand and helping her out of the car.

"What do you mean?" she asked, cooling off a bit as she shut the door and manually locked the vehicle.

"At some point," he replied, leading her to his Jeep, "Anders and I want to return to Denver to set up a medical practice. And in your case, your brother and grandmother have made Colorado their home. Maybe Callista and Anders were simply researching opportunities—for the future," he emphasized.

She didn't answer.

He opened the passenger side door for her. She sank into the seat, simmering with anger.

Or maybe she wasn't angry.

As he put her bag in the back with his, he caught her reflection in the rearview mirror. The fury in her expression had quelled, and heartbreak registered on her face. She was hurting. The muscles in his chest tightened. Yes, they went back and forth, tossing verbal barbs at each other, but he hated to see her like that. He got in the car and turned to her, but before he could speak, she huffed and started rooting around the console.

"Where's your charging cord? My mobile is officially dead," she barked just as his phone pinged. "Is it Anders?" she asked, practically vibrating.

He retrieved his cell from his pocket and stared at the screen. "Yeah, he's texting me." He held the phone, so she could read the message.

Anders: I need you to do me a huge favor. Tell me you're still at Helping Hands. I tried to call but got a message that they'd shut down early.

"Text him back and ask him if he's brainwashed Callista," Calliope demanded.

Alec pinched the bridge of his nose. "I'm just going to answer him like a non-lunatic."

Alec: I'm still at Helping Hands. Just getting into my Jeep to head to Rickety Rock. Calliope's car is giving her trouble, and she's riding me.

Riding me?

Jesus, what a typo.

"Fix it," Calliope demanded.

Alec: She's riding WITH me. Of course she's not riding me. I'm not a

His mind went blank. He glanced at the rec center and spied the outdoor Christmas display with a sleigh and . . .

"Reindeer!" he exclaimed. He hammered out the word, then hit send.

He reread his sent text.

Shit.

Alec: She's riding WITH me. Of course she's not riding me. I'm not a reindeer.

Calliope frowned as she stared at his ridiculous reply. "Stop the bloody reindeer games and tell him we spoke to Ralph and Louise and we need answers."

"Sorry about the reindeer flub. I'm concerned about Callista and Anders, too, and *reindeer* was the first thing that popped into my head," he muttered as he typed a new message.

Alec: We need to talk about

He got out the partial text, but before he could finish and hit send, another message from Anders populated.

Anders: A man should be pulling up with a delivery. It was supposed to be ready a few days ago, but it wasn't. The owner said he'd deliver it to you so you can give it to me.

Alec: What the hell is going on? What kind of delivery? And by the way, Louise and Ralph said—

A text popped up, and Anders cut him off again.

Anders: I've got to go. I'm trying to catch Raz when nobody's around, which is proving harder than I'd thought. Drive safely. The snow is really coming down. And no matter what, don't open what's about to be delivered. It's a surprise. See you soon. I'll let everyone know Calliope's riding up with you.

Alec turned to Calliope just as a sedan sailed into the parking lot. The man driving the car waved and pulled into the spot next to them.

"That's got to be the bloke. Roll down your window," Calliope instructed.

"You must be Alec. Merry Christmas Eve!" a stout, bright-eyed man with large ears sing-songed as he got out of his car and adjusted a pair of wire-rimmed glasses. Wearing a fuzzy green sweater and Santa-red pants, the guy looked like he'd been cast as one of Kris Kringle's elves.

"Anders . . . my brother . . . delivery," Alec got out like a Neanderthal. Between his texting debacle and this mystery gift delivery, he'd been thrown for one hell of a loop.

The elfish man's face lit up. "Please tell your brother we're sorry it took a few extra days, but we needed a little extra time in the workshop." The guy handed him a red gift bag with a mistletoe sprig printed in the center and four words emblazoned below it. "Enjoy the magic of the season. Anything can happen on Christmas Eve," the man said before returning to his car.

Why the hell was everyone talking about Christmas magic?

"Oh no," Calliope breathed as she stared at the bag.

He followed her gaze. Oh no was right.

Despite being delivered by a man who could easily play the part of Santa's head elf, this present hadn't originated in the North Pole. Whatever was in this bag had come from a place called *The Crystal Creek Jeweler*.

Chapter Three

Calliope Cress

In the glow of the Jeep's vanity light, Calliope stared at the sparkly thing, then shut her eyes. She mouthed the first few lines of "Frosty the Snowman." She didn't sing the whole song, because in her current state of absolute rage, she couldn't recall what came after the 'two eyes made out of coal' part. Harnessing her furious energy, she wished away the object, then opened her eyes.

"Bollocks!" she mumbled and glared at the diamond ring.

Yep, that's what was in the red mistletoe bag.

And it wasn't any old ring.

It could only be one kind of ring. With a single glittering diamond and the initials *AL* and *CC* engraved on the inside of the band, it had to be an engagement ring. The damn thing had taunted her from the second Alec handed her the bag and told her specifically not to open it. Who did the man think he was dealing with? She'd dived in with gusto, tossing red tissue paper like a kid on Christmas morning hopped up on caffeine and sugar. Oh, she understood she wasn't supposed to look. She'd read the bloody text, too. But come on. After a jewelry store elf delivered a little shiny mistletoe bag with a ring-sized red velvet box nestled in a sea of scarlet tissue paper, there was no way she could stop herself from peeking inside.

Honestly, part of her wasn't surprised. She'd be lying if she said Callista's smile didn't brighten every time Anders entered the room. Still, another part of her—the protective sister part—wanted to take Anders Lamb and roast his chestnuts over an open fire, and Alec's, too, for that matter. Those damned Lamb brothers had thrown a wrench into her life.

And speaking of a damned Lamb brother, she and Alec had barely spoken a word to each other since she'd cracked open the box.

Alec huffed for what had to be the millionth time. He'd been acting like Dr. Stick-Up-His-Arse for the whole drive.

She held the tiny box a few inches from his ear and snapped it shut.

That got her another huff.

She slapped a smirk on her face. "Do you have something to say, Alec?"

He tightened his grip on the steering wheel. "You've been mumbling for the better part of the last three hours. It's infuriating. Not to mention, you can't wish something away with a cheesy Christmas song. That's not how reality works. And even if it did, I doubt the lyrics to 'Frosty the Snowman' would be the key to unlocking the ability to teleport matter."

She felt her cheeks heat. "Was I singing aloud?"

"You've muttered that damned tune one hundred and sixty-nine times."

Her jaw dropped. "With your crazy propensity to eat like a woodland badger, I knew you were a food psychopath, but blimey, you're a Christmas-song-counting psychopath, too."

"Do you know what woodland badgers eat? Do you even know what one looks like?" he shot back.

Bollocks! She had no bloody idea. She fidgeted in her seat. "I was trying to make a point."

"And I was trying to keep my mind off . . ." Alec began, but he didn't finish. A muscle twitched in his jaw. The guy looked like one of those Jack-in-the-Box toys, coiled and ready to explode. He kept his gaze on the road as the wipers squeaked a frantic rhythm against the windscreen, and the blitzing snow swirled in the headlamps. The beams of light cut through the empty darkness, and it was like they were the only two people on the planet.

Here's the thing: She didn't need him to finish his thought. She knew the answer, and there wasn't enough spiked eggnog on the planet to numb the shock.

Anders would be proposing to Callista over the holidays. There was no other explanation. Still, a flurry of questions bombarded her mind.

Did Callista know Anders would be popping the question?

Had her sister and the bloke discussed marriage?

Those were pertinent questions and deserved answers, but they weren't the questions that shattered her heart. What she wanted—no, what she needed—to know was why Callista hadn't told her that things had gotten serious with Anders. Was she no longer her sister's closest confidant? Had a man who happened to be the mirror image of Alec taken her place?

She slumped forward, feeling the weight of the red velvet box in her hands, then placed it into the bag at her feet. It was time to zone out. She let her vision blur as she stared into the darkness. Between towering evergreens lining the narrow road and the headlamps picking up the swirling snowflakes, it looked like they were watching one of those old tellies when the signal got interrupted and the screen became a mess of black and white static.

She looked over her shoulder. They hadn't passed another

car since they'd left the main highway to traverse the mountain road toward Rickety Rock.

"For the record," Alec grumped, "we weren't supposed to open the box. I handed it to you to *hold*."

He did not get to play the part of the poor innocent bystander. "Bugger off, Dr. Wanker," she chided. "You were practically sniffing the bag the second that elf of a jeweler pulled out of the lot."

"It might not be what we think it is," he offered.

She huffed her amusement. "What else could it be?"

He shrugged. "A friendship ring."

"A friendship ring?" she exclaimed, shaking her head. "Are you completely off your rocker, Alec Lamb? It's an engagement ring."

Alec turned to her and parted his lips, most likely to continue arguing, when a flicker of movement in the great dark expanse caught her eye. She gasped as the beams illuminated a large form with giant horns.

"Alec, look out!" she cried.

"What is that?" he exclaimed.

"I don't think it's a bloody woodland badger," she cried. "It's enormous!"

The man cut the wheel sharply. They swerved to the right and then to the left, dodging the beast. But before she could take a breath, the Jeep hit a patch of ice. The car spun like a drunken ballerina. It careened off the road, wheels grating as they skidded along. Her heart hammered, and the roar of blood whooshing in her ears melded with the crunch of snow and gravel grinding beneath the wheels. Just when she thought her heart might explode, they jolted to a jarring stop.

She blinked, then surveyed the scene. The headlamps' light burrowed into a white wall where the snow had packed into an embankment. They'd landed in a shallow ditch. Her hands trembled. Her mouth went dry. She sat there dumbstruck as the click of a seat belt disengaging came from somewhere in the car.

"Calliope, Calliope!"

Somebody was calling to her, but her hammering heart muted the sound.

"Calliope Cress, I need you to say something. Talk to me."

Little by little, she returned to herself, and a dreamy awareness dawned. She turned toward the source of the sound. "Dr. Wanker? I mean, hi, Alec."

He leaned over the console and got in her face. "Are you hurt? Did you bump your head? Wiggle your toes. Can you move them?" he barked like a drill sergeant.

Still groggy, she complied, then cocked her head to the side as irritation edged out confusion. She wasn't wearing any knickers. She could not perish pantyless in the middle of Nowhere, Colorado, like some common Christmas harlot.

She inched forward, and the tip of her nose brushed his. "Alec Lamb, I cannot bloody die with knickers in my pocket. What the hell kind of driving was that?"

"It wasn't my fault. Whatever that animal was, it came out of nowhere. Let me look you over," he said, unbuckling her seat belt. He grabbed something from inside the console and blasted a beam of light into her left eye.

She reared back. "Are you trying to blind me?"

"I'm checking your pupil reactivity."

She waved him off. "I don't need looking over, Dr. W—"

Before she could complete the insult, he dropped the penlight and cupped her face in his hands. "I get it. I'm a bloody wanker," he said, doing a piss-poor job of speaking with a British accent. She was about to tell him he sounded as British as Yankee Doodle, but he tightened his hold. "I'm relieved you're okay. That could have been bad. There's nothing for miles. If you'd gotten hurt, I . . ."

There was panic in his voice. Sure, the guy could come off like a know-it-all, but that was his pragmatic side. At this moment, stranded on the side of the road, he was well and truly concerned about her.

"I'm okay, Alec," she said, retracting her verbal claws. Her chest heaved, and her fingertips tingled. In a state of shock, adrenaline coursed through her veins.

Maybe he was right to be worried about her.

"I want you to take three slow breaths, Calliope. I'll do it with you." Cast in the visor's dim light, his expression softened.

She stared into his eyes, inhaling and exhaling in time with him. Forget the near-brush-with-death business. This quasi-tantric breathing exercise was quite erotic. She touched his cheek. "Are you all right?"

He swallowed hard. The man was clearly still shaken. "That spin couldn't have lasted more than two or three seconds, but all I could think about was . . ."

The dim light warmed his chiseled features, and the man radiated an intensity that captivated her. He was a beautiful man. There was no getting around that. He drank her in with his amber eyes, and she released a shaky breath that had nothing to do with almost plowing into a buffalo or nearly taking out an over-sized woodland badger—or whatever the hell roamed the snowy mountainous terrain. Now, the rush surging through her veins had nothing to do with almost meeting her maker. She bit her lip, attempting to quell her arousal.

"Calliope," he breathed, and never had four syllables contained so much raw emotion.

Her body ached for his touch. "Yes?" she barely got out.

"We're not close to the edge of a cliff, are we?"

Good question. It was worth double-checking.

She flipped the visor closed and surveyed the dark terrain. "It appears we're wedged in a ditch."

"A ditch?"

"I don't see a cliff." She squinted. "There might be a structure back in the forest, but it's so dark, it's hard to tell."

He lowered the visor. The glow of light returned, and in the slip of time it took for her to look out the window, his gaze had grown positively carnal. "I know you said you didn't want to hook up anymore, but I've got to do this. I can't stop myself."

"What do you want to do?" she asked, hoping with all her heart it involved their naughty bits.

"I'm going to kiss you in a ditch," he announced. And as weird as that sounded, and despite telling herself she could not fall under his spell, it also felt like the only reasonable option under the circumstances.

"Yeah, okay," she replied, obviously not thinking clearly but lucid enough to know she wanted this man's lips attached to hers.

He leaned in closer, and she inhaled his scent—minty and clean, like sexy antiseptic—which also sounded insane, but it really got her going. He stroked his thumb across her bottom lip, teasing her, and a delicious flicker of heat sparked between her thighs.

"Alec," she whispered, and damn the man for having such a sexy name.

They stared at each other like they didn't quite recognize who they were looking at anymore. Were they friends? Were they foes? Were they simply shag buddies?

Two minutes ago, she would have called him her live-in booty call. But that no longer felt like an accurate description of their situation—especially when he looked at her like this and the lust in his eyes gave way to a deep, soulful longing.

The breath caught in her throat as he captured her mouth,

owning her with every kiss. There was no warmup. The man blew past giving her a little peck here and there. He wasn't nibbling. He was feasting on her. This man was in it to win it, kissing her like he was born to do nothing else. In a wild tangle of lips, teeth, and tongues, they kissed like kissing was on the brink of being outlawed. She needed to be closer to him. With the grace of an inebriated giraffe, she scrambled over the console.

Beep, beep, beeeep!

"Bloody horn," she moaned as her bum bumped the steering wheel.

But Alec didn't seem to notice. He growled against her neck. "I cannot get enough of you."

The feeling was mutual.

And then she remembered she was missing an item of clothing. She straddled him and rocked her hips, grinding against him pantyless and embracing her common Christmas harlot status. And oh yes, she'd gone full-on harlot. She was already wet—so wet. Alec had to be able to feel her through his thin scrubs.

He inhaled a sharp breath.

Yep, he knew.

Alec claimed her lips and kissed her with an intensity that— had she been wearing underwear—would have melted them clean off her body. And heaven help her. This man could lock lips. With surgical accuracy, that tongue of his had her moaning. They kissed with a fury reserved for long-lost lovers reuniting or soft-core porn actors hamming it up for the camera. Thanks to her commando status, they were probably more in the soft-core porn ballpark, but one thing couldn't be denied: this was not for show. The attraction between them was undeniable. Simply put, they couldn't get enough of each other.

He reached beneath her skirt and gripped her bottom with

both hands. "It should be against the law to have an ass this perfect. Oh, the things I want to do to you, Calliope Cress."

She arched into him as a dizzying current raced through her body. "I might have to stop calling you Dr. Wanker and start calling you Dr. Dirty Talk."

He ran his tongue across the seam of her lips. "Paging Dr. Dirty Talk. I like it," he purred, his voice becoming gravelly as he tightened his hold on her.

Bodies writhing and heated breaths mingling, they dry-humped like horny teenagers. The rush from their close call had ushered in a relentless passion that had her panting and desperate for Alec to fill her to the hilt with his glorious cock.

"I want you, Calliope. I never want to let you go," he bit out before releasing a guttural, animalistic growl. He was a growly, persnickety guy, for sure, but that sound was new—and so was the admission. He'd never said anything like that.

I never want to let you go.

His heated utterance carried an unwavering determination that heightened her need to feel the weight of his body pressed to hers.

Could he have meant it—really meant it?

Then again, they'd just experienced a brush with death. Perhaps he'd gotten caught up in the moment and the noise was a new so-glad-we-still-get-to-bang-each-other's-brains-out growl.

She closed her eyes, pushed aside his words, and prepared to get her snow-ditch freak on, when she heard the throaty grumble again.

Er, er, er, errrr.

"Is that you?" he asked as he kissed the sensitive skin beneath her earlobe.

She froze mid-hip thrust and pulled back. "I thought it was you."

She held his gaze as a prickly sensation hit.

They were being watched.

She turned toward the window, feeling like she'd landed smack-dab in a Christmas thriller. And—just as one would do in a Christmas horror flick—she shrieked and totally lost her shit. "What kind of bloody creature is that?" she exclaimed as a giant snout pressed against the window and smeared its gross snout juice across the glass. "That is no bloody woodland badger. What's coming out of its nostrils? Is that thing liquifying right in front of us?"

Alec inched away from the window, taking her with him. "Whatever it is, it's breathing hard."

"Damn the Wild West!" she cried. "I could be safe in the UK noshing on sticky toffee pudding. But no. I'm here, stranded on the road, and about to be ravaged by a bloody peeping Tom Buffalo."

The beast moved back a few inches and watched them curiously, like they were an exhibit in a zoo.

"It might be a bull elk," Alec offered, observing the creature, when a sharp knock pulled their attention to the passenger-side window.

"It's not a bull elk. It's Comet, the reindeer," came a muffled woman's voice.

Comet the reindeer?

Had they fallen through a rip in the universe and ended up at the North Pole?

"Who the bloody hell is that?" Calliope cried. "Where the hell are we, Alec?"

Dr. Dirty Talk tried to speak, but nothing came out. The guy was as gobsmacked as she was.

She couldn't see who was out there, thanks to the visor lights illuminating the passenger-side window. All she saw was their reflection until a beam of light sliced through the glass.

"Are those aliens?" she demanded, shielding her eyes.

"Crazy Americans are always on the telly ranting about being abducted from the middle of nowhere. I never believed it until now."

"It's got to be a flashlight," Alec answered, but the bloke didn't sound all that sure.

Whatever the source of the light, she'd be seeing spots for days.

The beast at the window lumbered in front of the Jeep, and the light from the torch vanished.

"Ho, ho, ho! It looks like we've got a couple of naughty-listers here, Mrs. K," came a man's warm voice infused with a comforting jovial quality.

"That it does, Nick, dear. That it does," the woman answered.

Naughty-listers?

They really had fallen through a tear in the universe and landed smack-dab in a bizarro Christmas world.

No, that was insane and impossible.

She needed to see what they were up against.

Drawing upon the nimbleness of a beached whale, she flopped from Alec's lap onto the passenger seat. With the same grace, she smacked the visor closed, then saw two older adults dressed as Santa and Mrs. Claus. The couple were dead ringers for the fictional festive characters. Decked in puffy coats and wooly mittens, the man waved as the woman held up a plate of cookies.

If they were getting abducted by Christmas aliens, at least there'd be snacks.

She rolled the window down an inch. "Who are you people?"

"Ho, ho, ho! We're the Krangles," the man announced warmly.

"*The Kringles?*" Alec repeated.

The white-bearded man chuckled, and his whole body jiggled like a bowl full of—that's right—jelly.

"We're not the *Kringles*," the cookie lady corrected. "We're the *Krangles*. Swap the *I* for an *A*, and that's us. I'm Noreen, and this is my husband, Nick."

This had to be a joke. And who knew Mrs. Claus had a first name?

She turned to Alec. "We haven't been abducted by aliens. We're dead. We're dead, and this is where people go when they die on Christmas Eve."

"I can promise you, you're not dead," Mr. Krangle answered. "But the temperature is dropping, and you could be dead very soon if you don't take the proper steps."

Holy shit! This had gotten creepy fast.

She was about to tell Alec to hit the gas and ditch the ditch when the reindeer lumbered up to the window, stood between the Krangles, and grunted. The old man released another bowl-full-of-jelly laugh, then pulled a freaking carrot from his pocket and fed it to the beast.

She'd nearly forgotten about the wild animal.

"Is your reindeer okay?" Alec asked as the creature chomped away.

"He's just dandy," Mr. Krangle replied and patted the animal on its giant head.

"Comet is our excitable boy, aren't you?" Mrs. Krangle remarked—like there was nothing totally bonkers about this situation.

"Can't blame him, though," Nick Krangle continued. "It's a special night. Children all over the world are waiting for him."

Holy holly and the ivy. These people really and truly believed they were Santa and Mrs. Claus.

Alec reached for his seat belt. "If everything's okay with your reindeer, we'll be on our way."

A smile spread across Mr. Krangle's face. "No, you won't. You're not going anywhere."

Chapter Four

Calliope Cress

Why would this carbon copy Santa tell them they couldn't leave? What the hell was this Christmas crazy talk?

She leaned toward Alec and lowered her voice. "Is this the American Christmas version of a serial killer movie? Are they about to throw us into a dank dungeon?"

Mr. Krangle knocked out another ho-ho-ho of a laugh. "You are quite imaginative. We don't have a dungeon, young lady. This is Mistletoe Manor."

"That literally means nothing to me," she answered, eyeing the penlight. If need be, they'd have to defend themselves with the ridiculous implement. She was about to go for it when Mrs. Krangle cleared her throat.

"My dear husband is simply trying to convey that the road is closed ahead," the woman reported.

"Should we go back to Denver?" Alec asked in a voice that said *please, for the love of God, say yes.*

Before Calliope could answer, the cookie lady shook her head. "That's not an option either. The road is closed a few miles back due to the icy conditions. You're stuck here for the night."

Oh, hell no!

"We have to spend Christmas Eve in a ditch?" Calliope shrieked, her voice rising an anxious octave.

Alec retrieved his mobile and studied the screen. "These people are telling the truth. Highway patrol shut down Route-Twenty-Four because of icy driving conditions."

She was ready to lose it and really throw a wobbly.

The road was closed. They were stranded in a remote slice of treacherous mountainous terrain, and there appeared to be a very good chance they were in the company of sugarplum-loving psychopaths.

It was time to drop a little East London attitude on these Yuletide yokels. "Listen here, boyo," she began, spreading it on thick as she eyed Mr. Krangle. "We're expected in Rickety Rock. Our families are there. They're waiting for us. And they will come looking for our bodies if we don't arrive on time. Also, my brother is a really big guy—like, massive."

God help her. She sounded crazier than the Krangles.

"Why don't you give them a call and let them know you're here," Mr. Krangle suggested with the twitch of a grin.

Now she felt like a right plonker. She lifted her chin. "And we'll be doing that—straight away."

"You're welcome to spend the night in Mistletoe Cottage. It's supposed to warm up tomorrow. I'm sure the roads will be open in the morning," Mr. Krangle said, then removed a fob from his pocket. He clicked it, and lo-and-behold, twinkling Christmas lights illuminated a cabin nestled among the evergreens.

"The guests we were supposed to host canceled last minute," Noreen Krangle explained. "The cabin is stocked and ready to give you the full Christmas Eve treatment. Mistletoe

Manor, the name of our place, is about a quarter mile down the road. We live there with the reindeer."

"You're lucky Comet stopped you. There's not another house for miles. You really could have gotten stuck out in the cold. But don't fret. While you won't have the company of your families, I believe you'll find Mistletoe Cottage quite inviting."

"And we've got top-notch Wi-Fi. It's a must in our business. We've got to be able to connect with the children of the world," Mrs. Krangle added.

Welp, these two were completely off their rocker, but cracking Wi-Fi was never a bad thing.

"Call your families and let them know what's going on. We'll meet you inside the cottage," Mr. Krangle offered.

"And have a cookie, my dears." Mrs. Krangle slipped two giant biscuits through the window slit before heading toward the cabin with her husband and Comet, the reindeer.

The trio trudged up a shoveled path toward the charming cabin.

Calliope looked from the cottage to Alec. "That can't be the real Father Christmas and his wife. If those people were who they said they were, they'd be at the North Pole. And I seriously doubt Santa rents cabins on the down-low in Colorado," she remarked, then concentrated on the sugary treats, laden with thick white icing and red and green sprinkles.

Her stomach growled. These biscuits could be laced with poison, but they looked bloody delicious.

Barely a second had passed before Alec's belly got in on the growling action. He eyed the iced delights. "Maybe they're holiday enthusiasts who enjoy Christmas cosplay."

It was possible.

"And the cookies?" she pressed as her mouth watered. "If they wanted to kill us, they could leave us out in the cold, right?

These must be safe to eat, don't you think? They sure smell like holiday heaven."

Alec stared at the cookie confection, and his belly let loose another rumble. "I'm willing to risk it. I'm starving." He plucked one of the cookies from her grip, took a giant bite, then melted into his seat with a sated sigh. "This might be the best cookie I've ever tasted," he said, humming his satisfaction through the bite, then stilled. He pegged her with his gaze as a sexy smirk graced his lips. "No, it's the second-best cookie I've ever *devoured*."

This bloody man.

She raised an eyebrow, but it was no use. She was too hungry to go toe to toe with him. "If I wasn't famished, I'd lob one hell of a retort at you, Dr. Dirty Talk."

"I know. That's what I love about us," he replied through another bite.

Love?

Her stupid heart skipped a beat. He didn't mean it like that —he couldn't. She should just eat the blooming biscuit and let it go.

She broke off a piece and popped it into her mouth. "Fuck me, it's absolutely scrummy." She sank into her seat as her taste-buds experienced a food orgasm. But before she could fall further under the sugary biscuit's spell, she bolted upright. "I meant *fuck me* as in this cookie is so good it's like a really great shag—like when we were in the laundry room, and . . ."

Gah! Had she lost her mind?

Alec took another bite, then flashed a cheeky expression. The man didn't utter a word. He didn't have to. She was doing a grand job of sounding like an idiot.

She broke off another chunk and eyed the morsel. She had to say something about the biscuit that didn't involve banging him. "It tastes like the cookie version of joy. If we're about to die at the hands of the cosplay Clauses, at least we'll depart this world with smiles on our faces." It was a bloody morbid statement, but it was better than sounding like she was a few slices short of a loaf of Christmas fruitcake.

Alec brushed a crumb from the corner of his mouth. "So we're agreed? We're spending the night in the Santa serial killers' cabin?" the cheeky bastard proposed.

A titillating zing zipped through her body.

With a dab of icing on his lip and a boyish grin slapped on his face, she was lucky she could coordinate swallowing the biscuit bite without choking.

Get it together.

"Call Anders," she said, all business, then took another giant bite of her cookie. Maybe an obscene influx of sugar would curb her libido.

Alec retrieved his mobile and put the call on speakerphone, but after one ring, it went to voicemail.

He lifted the mobile a few inches from his face. "Anders, it's me," he said, then glanced her way. "And Calliope. We've got some bad news. The roads are closed due to icy conditions, and there's no way for us to make it to Rickety Rock tonight. But we're safe. We're spending the night in a cabin near a place called Mistletoe Manor. Say hi to everyone for us. Tell them we're sorry to miss the Christmas Eve festivities. Give everyone our love. Hopefully, we'll see you bright and early tomorrow when the road opens." He ended the call and turned to her. "Did that sound all right to you? They'll know we didn't intend on spending the night together completely alone."

She nodded and tried to ignore the butterflies in her belly. "We're stuck and simply need a warm place to stay." Then again, they weren't completely alone. There were the mistletoe murderers down the road.

"This happened by chance because of the weather. It's not

our fault we can't get to Rickety Rock," he added, like he was working to convince himself.

She drummed her fingers on the dash as a realization hit.

Perhaps their current predicament hadn't happened solely by chance.

"Oh, bloody hell," she exclaimed.

He touched her arm. "What is it?"

"Could we have brought this on ourselves, Alec? We didn't kiss under the mistletoe at the community center. Ralph Dagby said that mistletoe doesn't forget, and Louise said mistletoe had the power to change everything. Could we have altered our destinies?"

Alec cut the ignition and turned off the headlamps. "I don't believe in stuff like that. We're here because of the weather," he said, looking away.

"You don't believe in fate?"

He fiddled with his keys. "I believe in science."

His words stung, and she couldn't understand why.

"Come on," he said. "We shouldn't keep the Krangles waiting."

She nodded because if she spoke, her voice might crack.

What was going on with her? The two of them had been shagging for months, and she'd never gotten sentimental over anything he'd said to her. What did she care what he thought about fate and destiny? She tried to shake off the feeling when the thought of being alone with him all night long had her heart racing like a virgin on her wedding night. She fumbled to open the door and bumped her foot against the bag with the ring.

The engagement ring.

No matter how she felt about that clusterfuck of a situation, she couldn't leave it in the car. She gathered her purse and the mistletoe bag as Alec grabbed their luggage. She exited the Jeep and almost fell over. Arctic air greeted her with an icy gust, knocking the breath clean out of her.

"It's colder than a witch's tit," she exclaimed, sounding like her granny. She'd only taken a few steps when Alec came to her side and draped his coat over her shoulders. "You don't need to play the gentleman," she said, waving him off.

But he wasn't having it. "Just wear it, Calliope the Christmas Commando," he teased, and a warmth settled in her chest. Unfortunately, it didn't radiate to her bare legs.

She hurried up the path alongside Alec and rubbed her hands together as the man opened the door. Even before she could see inside, they were met with a rush of heat and the comforting scent of pine and peppermint.

This sure beat freezing their arses off.

Alec brushed the snow off his shoulders, set the bags on the ground, then took their coats and hung them on a stand painted to look like a candy cane.

That should have been the first clue that their lodgings weren't your typical mountain abode.

She looked around, not sure if she could believe her eyes. It was as if they'd left Colorado and entered Santa's cozy retreat. If Christmas storybook charm was a decorating style, this place had it in spades. She glanced at Alec as they entered the living room area and caught the man wide-eyed. She couldn't blame him. The place was bloody inviting. A fire crackled in the cottage's hearth. Evergreen garlands lined with crimson ribbon wrapped around the cozy space, embracing the room. An expertly trimmed tree stood in the corner, with a train track circling the base. All she wanted to do was cuddle up on the couch and soak in the merry vibes.

Toot, toot!

She grabbed Alec's arm, then released a relieved breath when a toy train passed by on the tiny track. She leaned into him, comforted by his quiet steadiness, and inhaled another breath of peppermint-evergreen air. "This place is . . ."

"Christmas magic," Alec finished, wonder coating his words.

She kept an eye on the man as she rested her purse and the mistletoe bag on a little table near the door. She hadn't expected Dr. "I only believe in science" to react like that, but he exuded joy like a kid on Christmas. What had caused his demeanor to shift?

She chuckled, shaking her head at the man.

"What's so funny?"

"I didn't peg you as a Christmas enthusiast," she tossed back.

But before Alec could reply, footsteps echoed through the space.

Mrs. Krangle emerged from a hallway that led from the back of the cabin. "Oh, good! You made it. Welcome to Mistletoe Cottage. The tour is quite short. This is the family room and the bedroom. The couch is a sleeper sofa, but as you can see, it's rather large. Our guests tell us that it sleeps two just fine the way it is. I suspect there's a bit of cuddling involved to make it work, but you two look up to the task."

One bed.

Calliope nodded to Mrs. Krangle and studied the couch.

For as much sex as she and Alec had engaged in over the last few months, they'd never physically slept together. She assessed the sofa's overstuffed cushions and zeroed in on a quilt slung over the side. It was a delightful thing with stockings embroidered onto red and green squares. She clenched her core muscles. Her Dr. Dirty Talk could really stuff her stocking on a couch like that.

"What's that about stockings, dear?" Mrs. Krangle asked with a crease to her brow.

Oh, bloody hell! Had she said that aloud?

"Calliope, is everything all right?" Alec pressed, watching her closely.

"You were mumbling, dear. I couldn't quite make out what you said," Mrs. Krangle offered.

Thank God.

Calliope nearly breathed a sigh of relief, then made the mistake of catching Alec's eye. *Bollocks!* The twist of a smirk on his face indicated he'd been able to make out plenty. She shifted her stance, willing her cheeks not to burn with mortification. "I was admiring the quilt embroidered with stockings. It's lovely. Every stocking has a different toy in it. There's such attention to detail," she blathered like a twit.

"Aren't you sweet? I quilted it myself," Mrs. Krangle answered brightly, then waved them in. "And between the three of us, I have to admit I do love getting my stocking stuffed. Mr. Krangle is so inventive when it comes to stuffing a stocking."

Was this lady kidding?

"Is he?" Alec inquired.

Blimey! If Mrs. Krangle hadn't been there, Calliope would've kicked this git in the shins.

"Oh, yes," the woman trilled. "You should have seen the enormous gift he stuffed into my stocking last year. I can't wait to find out what he'll do tonight."

Sweet Jesus, make it stop.

"Jolly good fun getting stuffed on Christmas Eve," Calliope stammered and again made the mistake of glancing at Alec.

The man pressed his lips into a hard line, suppressing what had to be a full-throated belly laugh.

"What's down the hall?" she asked, changing the subject and praying there wasn't a room piled high with stuffed-stocking quilts. She'd never look at a stuffed stocking the same way again.

Mrs. Krangle clasped her hands in front of her. "The kitchen and the bathroom."

Hark the Herald! They were back on track.

If she didn't imagine Alec stuffing her stocking until she couldn't see straight, she'd be fine. She surveyed the room, admired the decked-out tree, then zeroed in on a wooden reindeer ornament. It reminded her of the flesh and blood reindeer who'd wandered onto the road.

"Where's Comet? Is he still outside? That can't be safe," she said and was met with Mr. Krangle's hearty ho-ho-ho of a chuckle.

The man walked toward them, coming from the back of the cottage, with a ruby-red shoebox under his arm. "Comet knows the way back to Dancer, Dasher, Prancer, and Vixen, Cupid, Donner, Blitzen, and—"

"Rudolph," Calliope supplied. She might as well play along.

Mr. Krangle frowned. "No, Frank."

She eyed the man. "You've got a reindeer named Frank?"

"Frank is our dog," Noreen Krangle answered, then tapped her chin. "And that reminds me. You haven't told us your names. We're not as familiar with the children on the naughty list."

Was the bad kid list really a thing?

"Oh, Mrs. Krangle," the Santa lookalike remarked, "of course these two are on the good list. Comet wouldn't have stopped them if they weren't."

This was getting weird—again.

"I'm not sure what list we should be on, but I'm Calliope Cress, and this is my . . ." She paused. Her what? Her fuck buddy from Denver? Her stocking stuffer? She felt her cheeks heat. What was she supposed to call him? "This is Alec Lamb," she finished, sticking to the basics.

"Are you a doctor, Alec?" Mrs. Krangle asked, taking in his attire.

The man was still in scrubs.

He looked down like he'd forgotten he was in his work clothes. "I'm training to be one. I'm in medical school."

"Isn't that a godsend, Nick?" Mrs. Krangle said, relief coating her words. "Show him what happened to you when you were handling your Yule log."

Holy Kris Kringle cosplay kink. Calliope had completely misjudged the Krangles. So much for luring them into the cute cottage to dice them into Christmas pie. These merry folk wanted to get their merry-Christmas freak on.

"I'm not sure I'm the right person to examine your husband's Yule log, ma'am," Alec stammered. He fiddled with the collar of his shirt as his cheeks grew rosy. "I'm in my first year of med school. I understand the basic biology and anatomy, but we haven't learned about treating Yule logs yet."

Noreen Krangle frowned. "I'm not talking about treating a Christmas Yule log. That's preposterous. A Yule log is a piece of wood decorated with greenery. I'd like you to take a look at Nick's hand. He hurt it while he was preparing the Yule log for the guests to burn in the cottage's hearth. It's a Christmas tradition, and he crafts them himself."

Alec exhaled a tight breath. "I thought you wanted me to . . ."

The woman cocked her head to the side. "What did you think I was referring to, young man?"

This was holiday entertainment.

"Yeah, Dr. Alec," Calliope asked sweetly. She batted her eyelashes at the doctor-in-training. "What were you thinking this nice Christmas lady wanted you to examine?"

Alec threw her a hefty helping of side-eye, and the breath caught in her throat. And there it was—that spark. Electricity pulsed between them. She lived to bust his balls, and with it being Christmas Eve, it was safe to say she also got a kick out of jingling his bells.

"Noreen, it's a tiny splinter, and you know I don't like going to the doctor," Mr. Krangle protested, holding out his right palm —a palm with a decent-sized, raised red bump.

Ew! It did not look good.

"It's inflamed and could keep you from your Christmas duties," Mrs. Krangle countered.

Alec's gaze flicked to the Santa lookalike's hand, and he pursed his lips. "Your wife is correct, Mr. Krangle. If the area is red and painful, it's smart to have it checked. Let me wash my hands, and I'll take a closer look. Take a seat near the Christmas tree. It's got the best light," he instructed, gesturing toward a small game table with four chairs.

Clearly, the doctor was in, and barely a minute had passed before the examination commenced. With the four of them seated, Alec and the Krangles focused on Mr. Krangle's hand, but that's not what grabbed Calliope's attention. She couldn't tear her gaze from Alec as he asked the man to describe his pain. There was nothing dismissive or condescending in her Dr. Wanker's demeanor. He listened, nodding while the man explained he'd noticed some discomfort last week when he'd been chopping wood for the Yule logs and then again felt the prick of pain when making toys for boys and girls in his work-shop. The old man sounded like a right nutter when he mentioned his hand also bothered him while he was preparing the reindeer for tonight's big event. Still, she could also see the color had drained from his cheeks. No matter who he thought he was, the poor bloke was in pain.

"It's your lucky day, Mr. Krangle," Alec said, gifting the Santa lookalike with a warm grin. "You might not be fond of visiting the doctor, so it's a good thing I'm just a doctor-in-training."

Mr. Krangle relaxed, and the rosy glow returned to his face. She couldn't deny her Dr. Dirty Talk had a brilliant bedside manner.

"Calliope?" Alec said, and Jesus, had her name always sounded so sweet when it fell from his lips? "Would you mind grabbing the first aid kit from my bag?"

The Calliope from five minutes ago would have teased him relentlessly for traveling with a first aid kit in tow, but not anymore. Observing him as he worked and seeing this side of him was like watching a picture come into focus—a picture she hadn't quite expected to see.

"Calliope?" he said gently—like his tongue and lips had been waiting for the moment they got to form the syllables of her name.

She pushed aside this new revelation and snapped out of her Alec-induced stupor. She found the kit and set the plastic container on the table next to the curious ruby-red box Mr. Krangle had been holding when he'd emerged from the back of the cottage.

What the heck was in there?

Before she could inquire, Alec turned to her. "Can you hand me a pair of gloves, two alcohol wipes, and the tweezers?"

Like a good makeshift nurse, she found the items and passed them over.

"Thanks," he replied, his fingertips brushing hers as she passed him the supplies.

And the butterflies in her belly were back.

Do not get all hot and bothered in front of the fake Santa people.

"What's wrong with my hand, doc?" Nick Krangle asked.

Alec slipped on the exam gloves, then used the alcohol

wipes to disinfect the tweezers and Mr. Krangle's palm. He probed the irritated bump. "You've got a splinter on the verge of becoming problematic. The good news is that we've caught it in enough time to ensure it won't get infected or impact your important duties. I'll remove the sliver, clean it, and apply antibiotic ointment and a bandage. In a few minutes, you'll be as right as rain, or in your case, *rein-deer*."

Sure, that was a corny-arse thing to say, but it was also a kind way to connect with the man and inject a little humor.

She opened the case and removed the ointment. "Here you go," she said, setting the cream and a small, circular bandage on the table.

"You two are a good team," Mrs. Krangle remarked. "And you've done my husband a real act of kindness. We're fortunate Mother Nature sent some weather our way and that our Comet wandered onto the road," she continued, as Alec attended to Mr. Krangle's hand.

"The magic of the season often has an uncanny way of delivering a Christmas surprise. This is the time of year when unexpected gifts often come our way," Mr. Krangle answered.

Noreen Krangle sat back in her chair. "I imagine you both thought you'd be doing something very different tonight."

It felt like a lifetime had passed since she and Alec had left the community center. "We did," she replied through a little laugh.

"The spirit of Christmas had other plans," Mr. Krangle offered, then tapped the box with his free hand. "Why don't you open this, Calliope." With a twinkle in his eyes, he slid the rectangular container toward her.

Ten minutes ago, she would have been ninety-nine percent sure there was a severed limb inside the box. Alec looked up, and she caught his eye. His playful gaze told her he was thinking the same thing. Now, she was pretty confident she wasn't about to encounter a dead creature or freaky Christmas voodoo doll. But that didn't mean she was about to whip off the lid like a magician's assistant.

Carefully, she lifted the top and—thank God—she wasn't met with a decaying squirrel corpse. What she'd uncovered was quite beautiful. The earthy scent of wood and fresh-cut greenery swirled in the air. She peered at the mound of leaves dotted with mistletoe. The festive rustic foliage sported a crisp gold bow that wound around a knotty white log. She touched one of the mistletoe's scarlet berries. "It's lovely. Is it a centerpiece?"

"It's a Yule log adorned with mistletoe," Mrs. Krangle answered. "Take it out of the box, dear. There should also be two slips of paper and two pencils on the bottom."

"Why do you include school supplies with the Yule log?" Calliope asked as she removed the elaborately decorated piece of wood.

"It's for you and Alec to write your Christmas wish," Mr. Krangle answered.

Alec glanced at the items. "How does it work?"

"You pen your holiday wish, fold the paper in half, then tuck it beneath the ribbon before you add the Yule log to the fire," Nick Krangle answered without an ounce of anxiety or trepidation as Alec continued to attend to his hand.

"It's a tradition to burn a Yule log on Christmas Eve," Mrs. Krangle continued. "The people who were supposed to be here tonight requested the romance Yule log. That's why this special log is adorned with mistletoe. It's said that a Yule log with mistletoe has the power to usher in true love. At least, that's what my mother used to say. Burning a Yule log decorated with mistletoe is how I ended up married to a man who made toys and raised reindeer."

Sure, the Krangles were bizarrely devoted to the whole

Santa ruse, but their love of the season was starting to grow on her.

"You wished for each other?" she asked.

"Not exactly," Mrs. Krangle replied with a wry grin. "Nick stopped by to visit my brother on Christmas Eve as my family and I were penning our Yule log wishes. I wished for love and adventure."

Love and adventure.

Could they go hand in hand? Calliope had always categorized them as a choice between one or the other. She'd never put them together. "Is that what you wished for, too, Mr. Krangle?" she asked, truly intrigued.

The Santa lookalike gazed lovingly at his wife. "My wish was a bit more specific."

"His wish was to catch me under the mistletoe," Mrs. Krangle answered with a little smirk.

Nick Krangle tossed his wife a flirty wink. "And my wish came true."

Calliope studied the Christmas couple. Warmth kindled in her chest, and she basked in their peppermint-scented affection. They might be lunatics who thought they were the fictional Santa and Mrs. Claus, but they were blissfully happy lunatics in love.

Would she ever experience a love like that?

She tucked the thought away.

Alec shifted in his chair. "Got it," he announced. He held up the tweezers and a decent-sized sliver of wood. "Mr. Krangle, you're splinter-free and cleared for Christmas merriment."

"I didn't feel anything. It's a Christmas miracle," the man exclaimed with a hearty chuckle as Alec finished up, administering the ointment and bandage.

"The real miracle is that we are all exactly where we're

supposed to be tonight," Mrs. Krangle corrected, meeting Calliope's gaze before turning her attention to Alec.

"Very true, my dear," Mr. Krangle replied. "The marvelous thing about this time of year is that the gift you didn't think you wanted is exactly what you need."

Could some sort of cosmic Christmas energy have orchestrated this odd turn of events? Was she meant to be alone with Alec on Christmas Eve? She glanced at the man and caught him watching her. And there it was again—those flitting butterflies in her belly. She felt a blush coming on, when a ho-ho-ho rang out. But Mr. Krangle wasn't the one doing the Santa laugh this time. She pinpointed the source of the sound and peered at a Christmas-inspired cuckoo clock on the wall with a jolly old Saint Nick's head popping out of a chimney as the clock chimed eight times.

"And now, we must bid you good night. Children from all over the world are expecting us," Mr. Krangle announced and helped his wife to her feet.

"But the road's closed," Alec remarked, pulling off the exam gloves as he glanced out the window. "And it appears to be snowing even harder than when we arrived."

The Krangles shared a knowing look.

"We don't need roads, do we, dear?" Nick Krangle said with a twitch of a grin.

"No, my rosy-cheeked love, we don't," Noreen answered and pressed a kiss to her husband's very rosy cheek.

Calliope and Alec trailed behind the Krangles as they made their way to the door.

"Thank you so much for allowing us to stay in Mistletoe Cottage. We're happy to pay for the night," Alec offered.

Mrs. Krangle waved him off. "We wouldn't think of accepting payment. You've tended to my husband's hand. We're in your debt."

But Mr. Krangle tapped his bearded chin like he had something up his sleeve. "There is one thing they can do," he remarked with a sparkle in his eyes.

"Name it," Alec answered, then took Calliope's hand in his.

Why had he done that?

A ripple of warmth passed through her as she twined her fingers with his. He brushed his thumb across her palm, and she inhaled a tight breath.

Did he even realize he'd reached for her?

Mr. Krangle glanced at their joined hands, then shared another knowing look with Mrs. Krangle. "Promise us that you'll look deep into your hearts before making your Yule log wish. Don't be afraid to dream big. It's Christmas Eve. Anything is possible."

Chapter Five

Alec Lamb

The cottage door closed, and for a beat, neither he nor Calliope spoke.

He glanced around as if he'd just woken up from a dream. "Did I just perform a minor procedure on Santa Claus?"

"Yes, and it was a smashing success," she answered. "Well done, you."

He couldn't hold back a grin as a soothing warmth emanated from his hand. He stroked his thumb across smooth skin, then looked down and had to do a double-take. He had Calliope's hand in his. And he didn't want to let go.

"I'm not sure how this happened," he stammered, holding up their joined appendages like a boxing ref signaling the winner. That boneheaded, gobbledygook of a statement had barely passed his lips, and instantly, he wanted to jam a half dozen of Mrs. Krangle's giant sugar cookies into his mouth to shut himself up.

What a moronic thing to say.

Calliope didn't appear fazed by his word salad of an explanation. She exhaled a shaky breath. Her boots clicked against the hardwood floor as she stepped back and broke their connection. Fumbling with her hands like she wasn't sure what to do with them, which appeared to be the theme of the last few minutes, she gestured toward the door. "Let's pull ourselves together. That couldn't have been the real Santa and Mrs. Claus because, well, there's no such thing as Santa, right? One guy and a bunch of reindeer could never make it to every kid's house in one night. It's like, science and shit," she blathered.

They both sounded like they were a few snowballs short of a snowman.

"It's a story meant to entertain children," he answered with a tad too much gusto, trying to ignore how much he missed her touch.

Why had he taken her hand in his? The truth is, he didn't know what had come over him. It happened like a reflex or magic.

Magic.

There was no such thing as magic, and there was no such thing as Santa Claus. He was a pragmatic guy, perhaps a bit of a killjoy, but he hadn't always been like that. And the part of him which had once embraced the wonder of the season couldn't help but acknowledge that it was rather remarkable that he and Calliope had ended up in this exact Christmas cottage on this particular night.

"The story of Santa and Mrs. Claus is a lovely tale," Calliope continued with a furrowed brow as she paced in front of the fireplace. "Even if they were real people, and we'd spent part of an evening with them, what kind of alias is Krangle? Calling himself Nick Krangle is a bloody daft way to hide his identity if he is the real Santa. Merging Saint Nick and Kris Kringle to come up with Nick Krangle is . . ." She paused, and her expression softened.

"Is what?" he pressed.

She blushed, and Christ, she was damned adorable. "I have

to take it all back." She gazed at the Christmas tree, and a dreamy expression took hold. "My head knows the truth about those people, but my heart wants to believe that there's more, that the possibility of something so wondrous could exist." She flitted her gaze toward the tree and touched the antler of a wooden reindeer ornament. "I'm not usually such a sap. That's Callista's department. She's the sweet one, and I'm the bitch. You must think I sound like a knob-headed prat."

He took a step toward her. "I've been with you almost every day for the last few months, but I'm still not sure what a knob-headed prat is."

Mischief sparkled in her eyes. "What about a wanker? Can you define that word, Dr. Wanker?"

A dizzying current raced through him. He tried to hide it, but he loved the feisty side of her. He parted his lips, prepared to concede he was familiar with the term *wanker*, thanks to a beautiful knob-headed prat calling him one nearly nonstop, but something from above caught his eye. More mistletoe. Who'd have guessed it?

She followed his line of sight. "It seems to find us, doesn't it?"

But he wasn't interested in the plant. He stared into her gray eyes and noticed something new. "They're a little bit green."

"What's a little bit green?" she asked.

"Your eyes. There's a whisper of green. No, sage. It's barely perceptible. But it's there." He cupped her face in his hands. A man could lose himself in eyes like this. "They're utterly beguiling."

She trembled beneath his touch. "I've got an identical twin, Alec. Callista and I share the same color eyes."

"That might be true, but hers don't call to me the way yours do. Your eyes tease me, they taunt me, they challenge me. They make me question everything I thought I knew."

He didn't usually talk like this. He wasn't a romantic by any stretch. He wasn't the type to moon over a woman, and yet, he couldn't hold back. Was it this place? Had the peppermint-scented cottage hypnotized him? Perhaps Mrs. Krangle had served them cookies with some sort of truth-eliciting ingredient baked in. Maybe the Dagbys and the Krangles were right in thinking that the magic of the season could do miraculous things.

Or was it her? Calliope Cress—the woman he couldn't get out of his head.

Whatever it was, it had left him enchanted and breathless as he drank her in.

A ghost of a grin pulled at the corners of her mouth, and he wanted to kiss her until he didn't know up from down or mistletoe from whatever the hell other plant had green leaves and red berries. It wasn't his fault he couldn't name one. He was training to be a medical doctor, not a botanist.

He dismissed all thoughts of plants and tipped her chin up. "I have it on good authority that it's a Christmas tradition to share a kiss beneath the mistletoe."

Unlike at the community center, Calliope didn't bolt. She pressed her hands to his chest and pushed up onto her tiptoes. "It would only be one kiss," she purred.

The sound of her sultry voice went straight to his cock. "We don't really have a choice," he conceded, leaning in, so ready to feel her soft lips, but the damned Christmas spirit had other plans. His phone pinged. The jarring sound pierced their dreamy, almost-mistletoe-kiss moment. "I should get that, right?" he rasped. His heart hammered in his chest, beating out a message telling him he should chuck the cell phone into the fireplace and get busy getting-busy with this enchanting woman.

Calliope chewed her lip, then dropped her hands to her sides. "You should answer it. It could be our families calling. We don't want them to worry."

She was right, but it didn't lessen the sting of disappointment.

Reluctantly, he searched his pockets for his phone. The buzzy energy popping and fizzing through his veins receded when he saw the identity of the caller. "It's your brother."

Erasmus Cress was great. They got along famously, and the boxing champion treated his sister like a queen, but that didn't mean he wasn't protective of his little sisters. He'd seen the man eyeing Anders when he was around Callista—and the guy wasn't smiling.

"Why is my brother calling you?" Calliope mused.

He stared at the tiny icon. *Shit!* "It's a video call."

Her rosy glow intensified into a tomato-red hue. "Answer it, Alec. We don't want him to think that we were about to . . ." She trailed off, but it didn't take a genius to fill in the blank.

They were on the brink of ripping each other's clothes off— for the third time in one day.

He plastered on a grin and accepted the call, but Calliope's beefcake of a brother's face didn't greet them.

A kid glared at him from the other side of the screen. "Oy, boyo," Sebastian, Calliope's seven-year-old nephew, barked in a surly British accent.

What was up with the kid? He and Sebastian had become great pals over the last few months. He loved spending time with him, but he'd never seen the boy like this.

"Hey, Sebastian," he said, treading carefully. "I thought your dad was calling me."

"Don't you 'hey, Sebastian' me, boyo. I'm using my dad's

phone. I need to get ahold of my auntie Calliope. She isn't answering her mobile, and Aunt Callista said she was riding with you to Rickety Rock. I don't know where she is, and that's your fault. You had one job, mate. Auntie Calliope is supposed to be here for Christmas Eve. We always spend Christmas Eve together, and she's not here."

The Cress family had spirit in spades.

"Your aunt is just fine, Sebastian. She's safe, and she's right here." He went to pass the phone to Calliope and found her sporting the same gruff expression as her nephew.

"Oy, boyo," Calliope shot back with a stern bend to her accent. "Is that how you talk to adults now? Granny Fin, your dad, Callista, and I taught you better, yeah?"

The boy's shoulders slumped. "Sorry, Auntie Calliope. I was worried about you."

"Come on, lad, you don't have to act like that," she said, her tone softening. "Now, apologize to Alec."

The kid mustered a weak grin. "Sorry, mate. I didn't mean to act like a right tosser."

Alec couldn't let the kid feel like whatever a right tosser was on Christmas Eve. He held the phone so both he and Calliope could be in the frame. "I get it, buddy. You care about your aunt Calliope."

"Of course he does. I'm his favorite aunt," Calliope teased, resurrecting a wry grin.

And then it hit. Alec must not have checked his voicemail. "Hey, Sebastian, did my brother mention that he got a message from me?"

The boy scrunched up his face, pondering the question. "I don't think so, but I haven't seen him that much. He's been in the den talking with my dad with the door closed, and before that, he was with Aunt Callista."

In the den with the door closed?

Ice prickled down Alec's spine. There was only one reason Anders would seek out a one-on-one with the boxing champion. His brother wanted to get the man's blessing.

"Have Anders and Callista been together a lot since you all got to Rickety Rock?" Calliope pressed.

Sebastian rolled his eyes. "Yeah, they're always together. You know how my friend Phoebe loves hot dogs?"

That was an odd response.

"Yeah," he and Calliope answered in unison, then traded confused looks.

"Phoebe says that Anders looks at Auntie Callista like she's a hot dog bun and he wants to be her hot dog."

Sweet Jesus! The kid had no idea how dirty that sounded. Calliope pressed her hand to her mouth to stifle her laughter.

"Why aren't you here yet?" Sebastian continued, bringing the phone closer to his face. "Did you stop because you had to pee? Phoebe always has to pee. That's because she started drinking chocolate milk every time she eats a hot dog. She eats so many hot dogs that she has to drink a lot of chocolate milk. She drank a gallon at lunch today, then burped, and it echoed through the whole house. She's blooming amazing."

This kid was hilarious. He had a sneaking suspicion that, in a decade or so, Sebastian would be looking at Phoebe like she was a hot dog bun.

"Why is there a fireplace behind you, Auntie?" Sebastian continued.

Calliope glanced over her shoulder. "We're at a place called Mistletoe Cottage. It's near Mistletoe Manor. We have to spend the night here. The highway patrol closed the roads because they're icy and too dangerous to drive on."

Sebastian pulled back the phone. The kid stared at them slack-jawed before his face lit up like they'd told him they'd hijacked a hot dog truck for his friend. "Mistletoe Manor?" the child exclaimed and set off, sprinting through the house. "Phoebe, Oscar, Aria! My Auntie and Alec are with the Krangles," the kid yelled, tearing through the old Victorian like a maniac.

What the hell?

Barely three seconds passed before the faces of four seven-year-olds crammed into the frame. It was his sister's friends' kids: Phoebe (the hot dog enthusiast), Oscar, and Aria.

"Do you know about Mistletoe Manor and the Krangles?" Calliope asked the smiling brood.

"Nick Krangle is Santa's best friend," Oscar answered.

"He helps Santa make wooden toys," Phoebe chimed, then lifted a hot dog to her mouth and took a bite.

"He and his wife have a reindeer farm. When Santa's over Colorado, he stops by Mistletoe Manor to let the reindeer play with the Krangles' reindeer and get a little rest before they visit the houses in North America," a gap-toothed Oscar explained.

"They've got a channel on the LookyLoo website," Aria volunteered. "We're watching their Christmas Eve livestream on our e-tablets. Look, their dog, Frank, is playing with Comet." The girl lifted a device and showed them a live shot of the Krangles in a barn surrounded by reindeer—and a dog.

Nick and Noreen weren't lunatics. They were Christmas social influencers. Now the bizarre behavior made sense.

He turned to Calliope. "And we thought they were serial killers."

"What did you say about the Krangles, Alec?" Sebastian asked with a thread of boyo energy.

Shit! He was met with four pint-sized scowls. For the second time today, it was a think-fast opportunity. "I said I forgot my *cereal chiller*. That's it—cereal chiller. Because I like my cereal very, very cold." His explanation was utter bullshit—more like reindeer shit—but it was the best he could come up with on the fly.

Sebastian pursed his lips. "I've never seen you chill your cereal at home in Denver."

"I do it in private," Alec blathered. Now he sounded as creepy as the Krangles did.

Phoebe pointed at the screen with the hot dog. "Is Alec all right, Calliope?"

Calliope patted his cheek like he was an amusing golden retriever. "Alec will be fine. I'll be sure to put his cereal bowl in the snow to keep it chilled. Now, where is Callista? Can you lot bring the phone to her?"

And the kids were off. The picture on the screen wobbled and blurred as Sebastian descended the staircase, and the hum of voices grew louder.

"There's Callista and Anders. They're sitting together on the window seat," Sebastian whispered, then turned the phone and gave them a view of the couple.

The kids had caught the pair in an intimate moment, seemingly unaware they were being watched. Anders had his arm around Callista's shoulders. With their heads bent together, they whispered to each other, smiling and giggling.

A warmth tinged with a touch of sadness washed over Alec. His brother looked happy.

"As you can observe, they're like a hot dog and a bun on a plate," Phoebe whispered as if she were narrating a caught-in-the-wild animal documentary.

"Sebby," Calliope chided, "stop spying on them and hand the phone to Callista, please."

For a few seconds, all they could see was the floor as the boy skipped across the room and handed the phone to his aunt. "It's Calliope and Alec," he said brightly.

Callista pressed her hand to her chest. "We just listened to your message a few minutes ago," she said, holding the phone so she and Anders could be in the shot. "I'm so sorry we didn't get back to you sooner. Anders was with Raz for the last hour or so. He'd left his mobile in the kitchen and didn't see the text come in."

His brother leaned in and blinked a few times, like he'd forgotten how video calls worked. "I was talking to the spiked eggnog, then we started drinking Erasmus," the man slurred. Jesus, the guy was plastered.

"Now that is being trolled," Calliope said under her breath. The woman was right.

Alec took in his inebriated twin. "Would you like to try that again?"

"Not really," Anders replied, grinning like an idiot.

"Raz and Anders might have overdone it on the spiked eggnog," Callista reported, smiling as she shook her head. She turned to Anders. "What were you two doing in there—besides knocking back far too much drink?"

Anders smiled a sloppy grin. "Talking," the man answered, then gazed into the camera. "Did you get what I need from the elf dude?"

He must have meant the ring.

Calliope pointed toward a table with the red bag and her purse.

Alec nodded to his brother. "Yeah, we've got it."

Anders clucked his tongue. "You looked, didn't you? I can read your face," his brother said, his sloppy grin widening. "You both saw it. You two are more alike than you think."

What did that mean?

Callista expelled a pouty breath. "Anders won't even give me a tiny hint about what he got me for Christmas. And I told him not to get me a present," she said, blessedly changing the subject.

His brother shook his head. "I keep telling you, *Lis*. I didn't get you a *Christmas* present."

Lis.

He wasn't so much of a Grinch to hear the adoration in Ander's voice.

Anders and Callista gazed at each other. And despite being plastered, there was no denying that his brother was head over heels in love. Oddly, Alec found himself feeling jealous of the man.

Where had that emotion come from?

Luckily, he didn't have time to answer the question.

A woman's voice with a rolling British accent pierced the air. "Are you talking to Calliope?"

Callista nodded. "Yeah, Granny, I'm on a video call with Alec and Calliope. The road into Rickety Rock is closed, and they won't be able to get here until tomorrow. Everyone, say hello to Calliope and Alec." Her sister turned the phone and panned it across the room, capturing the merriment. The kids zipped past the adults, who were chatting and laughing, as Christmas music played in the background.

"They're staying at Mistletoe Manor with the Krangles," Sebastian called.

Granny Finola entered the frame. "How'd you end up at a reindeer sanctuary?"

He and Calliope must have been the only two people on the planet who didn't know about the Krangles.

"We nearly hit a reindeer that had wandered onto the road. Alec's car spun out, and we ended up in a ditch. The Krangles came to offer help. But don't worry, we're no worse for wear, Gran. The car's fine, too."

"I'm glad to hear it," Finola replied, then pursed her lips. "And what an odd coincidence to end up at the Krangles' place. The kids can't stop talking about them. Those blooming people seem to be streaming on every electronic device in this house. Do they have you sleeping in the barn with the reindeer?"

"No, we're in a snug cabin on the property called Mistletoe Cottage," Calliope explained. "It's Christmas posh, Gran. You'd get a real kick out of it. The Krangles said we could stay here for the night."

"That was mighty kind of them," Finola answered, then narrowed her gaze. "Now, Alec?"

He swallowed hard. Finola Cress might be a granny, but the woman was damned formidable and a teensy bit scary—a lot like someone he knew. He glanced at Calliope, then directed his attention toward the screen. "Yes, Finola?" he eked out.

A crinkle of a grin bloomed on the old woman's lips. "I hope you're a good dancer, lad."

What did dancing have to do with being stranded in a Christmas cottage?

He frowned. "I'm not sure what you mean?"

"It's time for the Christmas Eve dance, dear boy. It's a Cress family tradition."

"Oh, Granny," Calliope fussed when the camera swiveled and the view changed.

Sebastian popped into the frame. "You've got to dance, Aunt Calliope. I know you like dancing with me the best, but you'll have to settle for Anders' brother. You don't mind, do you, Alec? Will you step in for me?"

The mention of touching Calliope had Alec's fingertips tingling. But he had to keep it together. He schooled his features. "I'd be happy to dance with your aunt."

"You've got to give me your word," the boy pressed. "And you've got to make Aunt Calliope smile. She always smiles when we dance together."

The kid had no idea how much he truly wanted to make

Calliope Cress smile. "You have my word. I'll make it my top priority to put a grin on your aunt's face."

"Do you think you're up to it?" Calliope asked in a sassy, trouble-maker tone.

"And you have to kiss her, too," Phoebe called, popping into the frame with a fresh hot dog.

Heat rose to Alec's cheeks. "Why would you say that, Phoebe?"

She gestured with her processed meat. "You're under the mistletoe."

He glanced up. Jesus, this stuff followed them everywhere.

Calliope plucked the phone from his hand and shook it like she was trying to scramble the circuits. "We're losing the connection. Hello, hello? Bugger all, it must be the snowstorm. We'll see you tomorrow." She ended the video call and released an audible breath. "That nephew of mine is a pushy little thing, isn't he? And Phoebe is a real piece of work." She handed him his phone, but she couldn't wipe the sweet as hell whisper of a grin from her lips. "We don't have to dance or . . ." She trailed off and gestured to the ceiling.

Or kiss.

He could fill in the blank. He could also sense the shift in her demeanor, and he didn't like it one damned bit. They were on the verge of a mistletoe kiss seconds before Sebastian called. He desperately wanted to return to that place where the world disappeared and it was just the two them. He wasn't about to let things get awkward. Luckily, he knew exactly what he had to do to get them back on track. It was a dangerous undertaking, but he didn't have any other choice.

There was no other way.

He had to piss her off.

Chapter Six

Alec Lamb

He schooled his features and braced for impact. "Are you a shit dancer or something?"

"Excuse me?" she shot back, wide-eyed.

"Listen, I gave Sebastian my word I'd dance with you," he said, adding a pinch of aloofness to his tone. "And that's what we're doing." He tapped the music icon on his cell phone and searched for a specific Christmas song. "Unless . . ." he added, then looked her up and down.

"Unless what?" she demanded, losing the air of anxiousness as she embraced her *boyo* bravado.

He bit back a grin. He had her hot and bothered and right where he wanted her.

Channeling his inner wanker, he returned his attention to his phone and pressed play. He pegged Calliope with his gaze as the first few jaunty bars of "Frosty the Snowman" rang out. "*Unless,*" he continued, "you need to know the correct lyrics to dance to a particular song, or you're just a shit dancer and you're embarrassed to dance in front of me."

That should do it.

Prepare for Calliope anger eruption in three, two—

"Nobody knows what comes after the 'two eyes made out of coal' part, you daft twit. We've already established that." She scoffed, then lifted her chin. "And I'm not embarrassed to dance in front of anyone. I'll have you know I'm a brilliant dancer. I've cut the rug to 'Frosty the Snowman' more times than I can count." She sized him up. "I can't imagine you've got any moves, Dr. Wanker."

A lightness took over. Going back and forth with this woman got his heart pumping.

He set his phone on the mantle. "I've got moves so hot, they'd leave good old Frosty a puddle of carrots and coal."

"I'll believe that when I see it," she murmured.

She took a step back, but he wasn't about to let her get away. In fact, she was about to see a whole different side of him. He reached for her hand and twirled her like they were auditioning for *Dancing with the Stars*.

Going round and round, she shrieked a playful girlish sound. "Bloody hell, Alec! What's gotten into you?"

He pressed his hand to the small of her back and twirled her body flush with his. She gasped, and he found himself breathless as the song ended. But they didn't stop dancing. He held her close and swayed his hips from side to side, doing a little step-step-together movement.

She rested her hand on his shoulder and glanced down at their feet. "Are we salsa dancing?"

"I'm not sure exactly what this dance is called," he conceded. "A couple of years ago, Anders and I were building a medical clinic in a rural village in Ecuador. This vivacious little old lady who lived on one of the nearby farms insisted on teaching us how to dance. I never thought I'd have any use for it, but it appears it was time well-spent."

Calliope relaxed into his embrace as a ghost of a grin graced her lips. "Why do you say that?"

"Because, Calliope Cress, my killer dance moves allowed me to fulfill a promise—a promise to make you smile." Just as the words fell from his lips, the palpable energy that drew them together shifted.

No, that wasn't right. It hadn't shifted. It had evolved.

A rosy hue warmed the apples of her cheeks, and he knew she felt it, too.

Curiosity glinted in her gaze. "Do you miss living in Ecuador?"

He cut out the fancy footwork, and they rocked gently from side to side. "I do. The people there are kind and hard-working. The food is amazing. Anders and I would spend half our day in classes and the other half building clinics or digging wells in tiny villages. It was always an adventure. What about you? You and Callista are world travelers. Do you miss teaching in South Korea?"

She nodded. "Like you said, going abroad is always an adventure. You not only learn about a new culture—you learn about yourself. You have to figure out who you are when everything in your environment changes and you're forced to adapt. Callista says we reinvent ourselves with every new place we go." At the mention of her sister, a pained looked flashed in her eyes.

He understood how she felt. His brother had been by his side through everything, and that was about to change. Still, there might be a silver lining to their situation. Perhaps their siblings weren't the only ones venturing down a new path. He and Calliope might also be on the cusp of reinventing themselves.

But first, he needed to know if she was okay with their sibling situation. "Any thoughts about Callista and Anders?"

She rolled her eyes. "Your brother clearly can't hold his drink," she replied, going into snarky mode. "That might be a problem for a man marrying a lass from East London. She'll constantly be drinking him under the table."

She was trying to keep it light, but he couldn't. He knew how much this affected her. "Do you think Anders wanted that alone time with Raz to ask for his blessing?"

Calliope sighed. "It makes sense. And from the amount of alcohol the two consumed, they must have been celebrating. We can try to deny it, but you and I both know that Anders is crazy about Callista and that she returns the affection. I'm sure my brother could see it, and I bet he appreciated your brother's gesture. It's old-fashioned but respectful, nonetheless." She paused. "Family is important to Raz. Our parents died when Callista and I were toddlers, and he became a father figure to my sister and me. When he won his first boxing title, he spent the money on us—on his family. He bought us a beautiful flat in a posh part of London and insisted on sending Callista and me to the best schools. That's the reason we decided to go into teaching. We'd been given so much. We wanted to give back. What about you? Why did you and Anders choose to study medicine?"

They hadn't talked like this before. Between screwing each other's brains out and trading barbs, he'd never entertained the idea that they had much in common. He was wrong.

He entwined his fingers with hers as they moved to the sounds of the crackling fire. "Anders and I want to give back as well. And it was important to us to honor the memory of our mom. Her doctors did everything they could to give her as much time with us as possible. We want to practice medicine and help those who need it the most."

"How did you lose your mum?" she asked softly.

"Cancer."

"That had to have been difficult."

"It was," he began, his voice thick with emotion. "Our dad

wasn't in a good place mentally after mom died. He pretty much checked out on us. That's when Libby stepped in. She worked a ton of jobs to make ends meet. We didn't have a whole lot growing up, but my sister always made a big deal about the holidays. She'd unpack all the Christmas decorations and turn every room in the house into a winter wonderland, like my mom used to do."

"Is that why you got all emotional when we entered the cottage?" She'd employed a teasing tone, but he could see the compassion in her eyes.

"I wouldn't call it *all emotional*," he lied through a smirk.

She cocked her head to the side, silently calling him out.

"Fine, I became *appropriately* sentimental at the sight of this place."

She rested her head against his chest. "I could tell something changed when you walked inside."

"It reminded me of my childhood, but that wasn't the only thing on my mind." A realization washed over him. The bullshit faded away, and he knew one thing for sure: the time with the people you cared about was precious, and one would be wise not to waste a minute of it.

"Are you concerned about the future? About what happens next?" she asked. "I knew it wouldn't always be Callista and me. But I'm the oldest, by seven minutes. I'm the planner, the doer, the type-A twin. I thought we'd have more adventures together before it ended. And I also thought that . . ."

He stroked his thumb across her palm. "What else did you think?"

Eyes shining, she looked up at him. "I thought I'd be the one to break away first. I always worried that Callista would have a hard time if I found someone."

It was like this woman could read his mind. He'd thought the same thing about Anders. "I get it. I'm the oldest—by four minutes. And we both know I can be a little rigid and anal retentive."

"A little?" she teased.

He chuckled. "All right, a lot. I'd planned Anders' and my future, too. I believed I had all the answers, but fate might have a different adventure in store for you and me. Maybe we're exactly where we're supposed to be. Maybe the mistletoe magic is rubbing off."

"I didn't think you put any stock in fate and magic," she challenged.

A warmth spread from the top of his head to the tips of his toes. "I didn't, and then we hit a patch of ice, and the first thought that came to my mind while we were sliding across the road was that I didn't want to lose you."

He wasn't the kind of guy who spouted his deepest feelings. But his admission wasn't sappy or over-the-top. It was the truth —a truth he no longer wanted to disregard.

Calliope's bottom lip trembled. "You hardly know me, Alec. When we aren't shagging, we're insulting each other. And half the time, we're shagging while trading barbs."

He could sense her vulnerability, and it gave him the courage to open his heart. He twisted a lock of her hair between his fingers. "That's not entirely true. I know you better than you think. I know you care about your family and children. You're protective of your sister, and I can't even count the number of times I've seen your face light up when you're with Sebastian. I know you're a damned good teacher. I walked by your classroom more times than I'd like to admit. Your students adore you. And the medical staff was talking about how their kids were thrilled to have you volunteering in the childcare center." He swallowed past the lump in his throat. The walls he'd erected around his heart had crumbled, and there was no holding back now.

"What is it?" she asked gently.

"There's more."

She held his gaze. "You can tell me."

Excitement and trepidation flowed through his veins. If Calliope's touch wasn't grounding him, he'd surely float away. He was the definition of punch-drunk.

He steadied himself. "I know that when you walk into a room, it takes every ounce of my strength not to gather you into my arms and never let you go."

"That's the second time you've told me you never wanted to let me go," she said as the warmth in her smile echoed in her voice.

She was right. He'd spoken the same words in the car.

He tucked the lock of hair he'd been playing with behind her ear and tightened his hold on her body. "When the car started spinning on the ice, fear gripped me like nothing I'd ever experienced. But I wasn't worried about myself."

She observed him closely. "What were you worried about?"

"You," he got out in a rasp of a breath. "I didn't want you to get hurt. When we started sliding, everything slowed down. Flashes of you came to me. I saw your face, your eyes, that sexy as hell twist of a grin, and then one thing became overwhelmingly clear. My feelings went beyond wanting to keep you safe. I felt something deeper, something that tapped into a part of me I didn't even know existed, and I can't ignore it any longer."

"What can't you ignore?" she asked, her voice barely a whisper.

"Love." The word fell from his lips like a flawless snowflake dancing in the air.

"Love?" she repeated.

He nodded. "From the moment I met you, I felt our connection. Even when you make me spitting mad, which you do a hell of a lot, I want to remain close to you. When I hear your footsteps, my heart races. When your voice carries on the breeze,

I'm drawn to you like a moth to the flame. You're the last thing I think about before I fall asleep, and when I wake up, you're the first thing on my mind."

"Alec," she interjected.

But he couldn't stop. "We make each other crazy, but we also challenge each other. We're good together in a train-barreling-down-the-tracks sort of way. Our passion and our commitment to the people we care about drives us. And Jesus, the chemistry between us is explosive. I even like it when you call me Dr. Wanker. If that's not love, then I don't know what love is."

That was one hell of a Christmas Eve confession. He'd put it all on the line. The snowball was in her court now.

For a beat, she remained silent, then the corners of her lips tipped into a devilish smirk. "What if I told you I had a thing for wankers?"

His heart hammered as a buzzy elation took over. "Are you saying you could love a wanker? Because we both know I'm off the charts when it comes to wankering."

"Two things," she replied, not missing a beat. She assumed her prim schoolteacher demeanor. "First, never say *wankering* again. It sounds bloody ridiculous."

He suppressed a grin. "And number two?"

"Understand this, Alec Lamb." Her expression grew earnest as she dropped her headmistress persona. "I couldn't see myself loving any old wanker, but it's quite possible that I'm already in love with a wanker doctor-in-training."

Excitement flooded his system. "Mr. Krangle did say anything was possible on Christmas Eve. And here we are, just the two of us—you and a wanker."

She stroked his cheek and chuckled.

"But I'll tell you one thing that's *not* possible," he added as his eye caught a flash of red and green.

She raised an eyebrow. "And what's that?"

He gestured toward the trio of leaves dotted with scarlet berries. "It's not possible for me to stop myself from kissing you. I have it on good authority that a kiss under the mistletoe can lead a person in a direction they never expected. What do you say, Calliope Cress? Do you want to chase the unexpected with me?"

In all his life, he'd never wanted anything more.

She gifted him with that mischievous twist of a grin. "I'm not sure I have a choice in the matter. The spirit of Christmas couldn't make itself any clearer. Sprigs of mistletoe have been hounding us all day, and I dare say, its magic has landed us here —in this unexpected wonderland cottage. The mistletoe's been trying to tell us something. There's a good chance, if we don't heed its call, we could end up on Santa's naughty list. We'll have to hope we don't kill each other in the process, but yes, Alec Lamb, I agree to chase the unexpected with you."

"I'm going to have to disappoint you regarding one of your assertions," he replied in a mock-serious tone.

"Disappointing me already? How very British of you. And what disappointment shall I prepare myself for?" she asked, mimicking his mock-serious tone.

His cock twitched. "After I'm done with you, the only list we'll be allowed on is the naughty one."

She swayed and brushed against him, rendering him rock-hard.

Her eyes widened. "I see the Christmas spirit has strengthened your resolve. You appear to be ready to stuff some stockings."

This woman.

He was near dizzy with happiness.

He eyed her appraisingly. "And you look like you're ready to have your stocking stuffed."

Calliope leaned in. "I have the feeling we'll never be able to look at Christmas fireplace decor the same way again."

He scanned the generic stockings dotting the hearth and shrugged. "I can live with that," he growled, then captured her mouth in a scorching kiss, hot enough to land them on the very top of the naughty list. He couldn't help himself. She tasted like sugar-coated forever, and he devoured her sweetness.

"Alec," she breathed between kisses, "I need you to do something for me."

"Anything."

She gave him the once-over. "Take off your shirt."

He wasn't expecting that. But he sure as hell wasn't going to say no. He held her gaze and peeled off his powder blue top, doing a scrubs strip tease.

Lust glittered in her eyes as the dirtiest expression bloomed on her face. "I thought you were hot in those gray sweatpants, but they don't hold a candle to you topless in scrubs. It takes my Dr. Dirty Talk fantasy to a whole new level." She raised her index finger. "But wait! I've got a naughty little move of my own."

He stepped back and crossed his arms. "Let's see what you've got."

She pranced around the room, then slipped her emerald panties from her pocket. Theatrically, she waved them over her head like a naughty cowgirl, then tossed them onto the tree. "It needed that," she quipped playfully before sauntering over to the couch. She turned her back to him and bent over. "Don't mind me," she teased. "I'm fluffing these cushions."

He didn't think he could want her more.

"I'm thinking about fluffing something a hell of a lot better than cushions," he replied, drinking in her beautiful bare ass.

She peered over her shoulder with a come-hither look in her eyes. "If the doctor is in, I'm ready to have my halls decked."

Damn right she was ready.

He came up behind her and brushed her hair over her shoulder. "Are we doing this while making terrible Christmas puns?" he asked and pressed a kiss to her neck. "Because I'm ready to jingle your bells."

"Look who's got a funny side," she replied, then moaned as he ran his teeth below her earlobe.

"I'm more concerned with your *backside*. Hold on to the couch. You'll want to brace yourself. Santa isn't the only one who'll be coming tonight."

Her body vibrated with laughter. "That's a good one."

He shrugged down his pants and boxer briefs and rubbed the tip of his shaft against her entrance. Her giggling ceased, and she inhaled a sharp breath as he pressed past her delicate folds. She was already slick with desire. Lust tore through him, and the urge to thrust hard and fill her to the hilt nearly took over. Yes, he wanted her. He wanted her so badly he could barely see straight, but tonight was special. He exhaled a slow breath and backed away from her.

Calliope peered over her shoulder. "What are you waiting for?"

He'd been waiting for the chance to have her for more than just a fast screw. They weren't hidden away in the pantry or banging against the bathroom sink. They had this cottage all to themselves.

He scanned the space and found Mrs. Krangle's plate of cookies on a side table. "Here, have a cookie," he said, and handed her one of the frosted treats. "And could you step back a few feet?"

With a furrowed brow, a perplexed Calliope accepted the cookie and moved away from the sofa. "Are we taking a snack break?"

He threw the couch cushions on the ground.

"Or a pillow fight?" she pressed through a bite, watching him like he'd lost his mind.

He pulled out the sleeper bed and adjusted the mattress. "We've got a bed, and dammit, we're going to use it," he announced, then pointed to it like he'd discovered the Eighth Wonder of the World.

She took another bite of the sugar cookie, then set the half-eaten treat on the plate. "I should let you in on a little secret about me and beds. You'll want to hold on to your stethoscope for this confession, Dr. Wanker. It might shock you," she purred, sauntering past him as she seductively ran her hand across the mattress.

"Let's hear it." Christ, he loved it when she teased him.

She slipped her shirt over her head and dropped it to the ground. "I'm very particular about one thing when it comes to utilizing a bed." She removed her bra and tossed it onto the tree. It hung next to her panties, creating the naughtiest set of tree trimmings he'd ever seen.

"Nice touch," he said with a nod to her undergarments.

She pointed to the bed. "Sit," she ordered.

Damn, he liked her bossy. He sat, happily channeling his inner golden retriever. Honestly, if she told him to bark, he'd throw open the window and howl at the moon.

She stood before him, lifted her leg, and pressed her booted foot between his thighs. "Can I get a little help with these?"

He went to work as if his sole purpose on this planet was to remove her footwear.

Boots off, she held his gaze and continued the strip tease. She hinged forward slightly, slid her skirt down her long, toned legs, then straightened to her full height. Like a beautiful temptress, she ran her hands down her torso and sighed a sexy little sound. "When it comes to beds, I like to sleep completely naked."

His rock-hard hard-on was full-on okay with her sleeping in the buff.

Play it cool. Channel Frosty.

He kept his expression neutral. "Funny thing about that," he replied, coming to his feet. He removed the rest of his clothing and stood before her, buck naked.

She raked her gaze down his body. "And what's that?"

"I also like to sleep completely naked."

"Aren't we well-matched? Or should I say mistletoe-matched?" she finished and pointed to the ceiling.

He peered at the sprig—the bit of green and red that had sparked the events of this life-changing day. "We're not just a mistletoe match. We're a mistletoe *love* match."

She rested her hands on his chest. "I like the sound of that."

"I like the sound of making you come more," he countered, then whisked her into his arms.

Calliope shrieked as he tossed her onto the mattress. Her hair fanned out in waves around her face, but he didn't join her —not yet. He paused. Surrounded by the scent of pine and peppermint, he surveyed the Christmas cottage and knew one thing for sure; their love story started here.

She ran her left foot down her right calf in a sensual, sexy movement. "Like what you see?"

"I love what I see." He fell to his knees at the end of the bed. Starting with her ankles, he kissed a trail up her calves, past her knees, and hummed his pleasure as he worked his way to her hot, wet center. He teased her with his tongue. "And I love how you taste."

She rocked her hips and tangled her fingers in his hair, writhing beneath him. "Better than Mrs. Krangle's cookies?"

He glanced at the plate piled with the frosted treats. "What cookies? There's only one cookie I want."

She gifted him with a sexy smirk. "Good answer."

He feasted on her body, then inched his way up her torso. He massaged her breasts, running his teeth along each tight peak, before licking a line to the hollow of her neck. He worked methodically. This was no furiously rushed fuck in a darkened closet. But make no mistake—he'd always be up for furiously fucking Calliope Cress. The mere thought of taking her hard and fast had his cock weeping.

But tonight was different.

Tonight, he could take his time and savor each point of contact. He reveled in making Calliope tremble beneath him, but there was only so much waiting a man could do with a beauty like this moaning beneath him. She arched her back and hummed her satisfaction, and he couldn't wait any longer. He thrust his cock inside her.

"It's so good," she whispered against his neck. "It's always so bloody good."

It was. It was like nothing he'd ever known.

It didn't matter how many times they'd come together as one. He was never prepared for the rush of lust and longing that took hold. But this time, he fought the urge to pump his hips until sweat lubricated his skin. He stilled and studied her face. In the space of a breath, every sensation intensified.

And he knew why.

Love.

A love steeped in Christmas Eve magic.

It was the gift he'd never expected that happened to be exactly what he needed.

He saw his life through a different lens. Sure, he was still Anders' twin brother, and the two would always share a bond, but now, his wanker heart belonged to Calliope Cress. Their relationship would no longer be relegated to stolen kisses and late-night rendezvous. Behind the back-and-forth bickering and late-night sexytimes, something miraculous had formed between them. And thanks to a hell of a lot of mistletoe, a layer of ice, and a wandering reindeer, their destiny had been revealed.

She was meant to be his.

Not even her trademark Calliope sass could hide the love shining in her eyes.

He took note of each freckle and relished the curve of her kiss-swollen lips. With her hands above her head resting on her tangle of thick locks and the scent of Christmas in the air, she was an erotic holiday goddess, beckoning him to make her cry out with pleasure.

"Alec," she said, calling to him like a Siren's song, and the syllables never sounded sweeter.

He gripped her slender wrists and pinned her to the bed. Lust welled in her eyes. She bucked her hips, and he knew exactly what she wanted. He worked her body in long, sensual strokes. The friction built between them as a spark ignited, and a firestorm of passion took hold. Each thrust propelled them closer to sweet release. He held her in place, controlling the speed and pressure. She was his to tease and tempt. Grinding his pelvis against her sensitive bundle of nerves, he let out a primal growl as she cried out, teetering on the cusp of oblivion.

Drowning in a sea of gray laced with swirls of sage green, he threaded his fingers with hers, holding on like he never wanted to let go, and in that sweaty slip of time, he made her a silent promise.

His heart belonged to her—it always would. The magic of the mistletoe would ensure it.

He dialed up his pace and pistoned his hips. Calliope was there, teetering on the precipice of pleasure. He could feel it. Before he could release another heated breath, she tightened around him and arched her back as she lost herself in the waves of pleasure. Carnal victory tore through him, and he let go.

Pumping hard and fast, he joined her, and they catapulted into a sea of desire.

They hovered in the space between this world and the next, and he whispered her name over and over like a prayer. "Calliope, Calliope, Calliope."

The slap of skin meeting skin dissolved into the peppermint air, and his pulse slowed as he wound down from the rush of release. He kissed her deeply and smiled against her lips as she hummed her contentment.

He was one damned lucky man.

He shifted his weight, rolled onto his side, and gathered her into his embrace. Basking in the afterglow of their lovemaking, he stroked her arm, lazily drawing his fingertips across her soft skin. He'd never pegged himself as a cuddler, but like everything else, he'd formed a new opinion on the matter.

She traced her fingertips down his jawline. "That, Alec Lamb, was a truly *adequate* shag."

How could a man not fall ass-over-elbow for this woman?

"Ladies and gentlemen," he said, mimicking a television announcer, "I bring you Alec Lamb: doctor-in-training and deliverer of truly adequate sex."

With naughtiness written all over her face, she pushed him onto his back, then rested on his chest. She tossed a sated smile his way and glanced toward the fireplace. "I need to get on that Yule log."

He reached between his legs and felt his cock—his very spent cock. He bounced back relatively quickly in the Yule log department, but it had barely been a minute. He cringed. "About the Yule log. It might need a minute—or ten. Ideally, twenty."

This earned him a full-on belly laugh from his British beauty. "Not *your* Yule log, Dr. Wanker. The real Yule log the

Krangles left us." She left their sex cocoon, shimmied on his scrubs top, and retrieved the items.

He found his bottoms and pulled them on, watching as she set the log, the paper, and the pencils on the table next to the plate of sugar cookies. "We're doing this now?"

"Why not?" she replied with a flirty half-shrug. "We have nineteen minutes to kill."

He plucked a sugar cookie from the plate and hoovered it in three bites.

She raised an eyebrow at him.

"Got to keep up my strength," he said through the bite.

She shook her head and handed him a pencil and a piece of paper. "Do you know what you're going to wish for?"

Hell yes, he knew exactly what he wanted. But that didn't mean he couldn't add a little suspense to the wish-making process. He turned away from her and sported a furtive expression. "It's a secret. No peeking."

"We already have secrets?" she lobbed back with a mock pout.

"We're already a 'we'?" he teased, loving the sound of it.

"You did proclaim your undying love and devotion and, thanks to a hell of a lot of mistletoe magic, I reciprocated. So yes, we are the *we-est* of *we's* now."

He pointed at her with the pencil. "Wait a second. You can say *we-est*, but I can't say *wankering*?"

She pushed aside the pencil and kissed the tip of his nose. "Welcome to being in love with Calliope Cress."

He cupped her face in his hand. "Well, Calliope Cress, the woman I love, humor me on this," he said, his lips millimeters from hers. "Let's keep our wishes a secret and see what happens. Think of it as our first adventure."

She pulled back a fraction and narrowed her gaze. "I'll agree if you promise me one thing."

He stroked her cheek, falling deeper and deeper in love by the second. "And what is this one thing?"

She owned him with her sparkling gray eyes. "Promise me you won't hold back. Promise me you'll do as Nick Krangle advised and dream big."

"I promise," he answered and pressed his lips to hers, sealing their agreement with a kiss. But she wouldn't have to wait long to find out if what he was about to write on the slip of paper would come true. The outcome of his wish was only hours away from being revealed. It all hinged on her, and the choice between yes or no.

Chapter Seven

Calliope Cress

Calliope sighed, savoring the warmth engulfing her body as she emerged from her slumber. She cracked open her eyes and was met with the image of a stocking stuffed within an inch of its life. "I absolutely know how you feel," she murmured to the quilt, her voice low and gravelly.

She batted away the blanket that had bloody ruined her when it came to Christmas fireplace decoration and gazed down at a large hand palming her left breast. A delicious tingle worked its way down her spine, and she hummed her contentment.

There were certainly worse ways to greet the day.

"Merry Christmas," came the voice of the sexiest doctor-in-training on the planet. "Are you awake?"

"I'm not sure. I might be dreaming." She shifted in his arms and met his amber gaze. "You see, I'm not in my bedroom. I'm in a Christmas cottage decked with mistletoe and my knickers hanging from a tree. And it appears I've woken up naked next to a man who drives me bloody crazy."

He ran his fingertips down her arm, then palmed her bare

arse. "I hate to break it to you, but you're not dreaming. You are, in fact, in a mistletoe-laden Christmas cottage. And yes, you've woken up naked and in bed with a man who drives you crazy. However," he continued, eyes sparkling, "this man drives you crazy in the dirtiest ways possible, and you're totally good with that. But there's more."

"There's more?" she repeated, playing along.

"It just so happens that you're completely and hopelessly in love with him."

"*Bloody hell!* I'm stranded in a Christmas cottage *and* in love with a wanker almost-doctor? It's a Christmas miracle."

Alec chuckled, then pressed a kiss to her temple. "Did you sleep all right?"

She arched her back and stretched like a sated kitten. "I did. The Krangles weren't kidding. This bed is bloody comfortable."

Alec narrowed his gaze. "You did hog most of it."

"Bollocks," she shot back. "If anyone is a bed-space stealer, it's you, Dr. Dirty Talk."

"Now it's Dr. Dirty Talk?" he purred.

Thank goodness she was lying down. Between the banter and this man's sexy morning voice, she'd gone weak in the knees. But who could think about knees?

She shooed away the thought and focused on his cock. She reached down and found him rock-hard. "I see the doctor is up."

Mischief glinted in his eyes. "I should let you in on something. That reaction is caused by an acute illness I suffer from."

She gasped dramatically. "What would that particular affliction be?"

"*Calliope-itis,*" he replied in a playfully grave tone.

"*Calliope-itis?* It sounds bloody awful. Is there a cure?"

He mustered a pained expression. "There is, but the cause is the cure."

"Interesting. Tell me more," she shot back, wide-eyed.

"Whenever a person named Calliope drives me insane, pressure builds in a specific part of my body."

She had a good idea of where he was going with this. "I'm guessing that pressure build-up occurs below the belt in the Yule log region?"

"You would be correct," he answered, sticking with his mock-serious tone. "And the only way to release it is to bang the hell out of someone named Calliope—hence, the name, *Calliope-itis*. Do you happen to know if there's a Calliope in the vicinity? As you can tell, I need to bang her until she can't see straight. It's not for any sexual intent, of course. It's a purely medical necessity."

She climbed on top of him and straddled his torso. "You poor thing. It's your lucky day—another Christmas miracle. My name is Calliope, and I could sure do with a before-breakfast banging. And with it being a special day and all, I can safely say that all I want for Christmas is *not* my two front teeth but for my wanker doctor to bang the hell out of me."

"One Christmas banging coming up," he growled, but a ping caught their attention. He glanced at the side table. "That's got to be the text."

The text? What text was he talking about?

He reached for his cell and tapped the screen. "Yep, there it is," he uttered with a cat-who-ate-the-canary expression.

"What are you talking about? Who's texting you? Is it Anders?" she asked.

He held out his mobile. "Ralph Dagby."

"Ralph bloody Dagby? What does he want?" And then it hit. "Blimey, I'd forgotten he'd mentioned texting us this morning." She skimmed the message. "He wants to know if we'd like to continue volunteering at Helping Hands."

The man said he'd ask for their answer today.

What was their answer?

Sure, she and Alec had proclaimed their feelings, but they hadn't discussed logistics. Did he want to go back to Ecuador? Did she want to return to South Korea? Would they try to maintain a long-distance relationship?

As if he could sense her turning over question after question in her head, he sat up, taking her with him, then halted her inner turmoil with a kiss. "It's a big world, and I want to experience it with you. But there's nothing that says our adventure can't start here."

The man had a point.

She wrapped her arms around his neck. "No, there isn't, and we really can't leave Denver at the moment," she mused. "Out of everyone in our families, we're the ones who keep this crazy Lamb-Cress train on its track. What would they do without us?"

He nodded. "It's an act of charity, really."

The truth was, she enjoyed living in Denver. She loved seeing her brother happy and in love, and she couldn't deny she'd missed being with Sebastian.

"I've got news for you, Calliope Cress," he added.

"And what news is that?"

"Our mistletoe love match isn't just a Christmas fling. I'm in love with you. But I can't have you sauntering under the mistletoe when I'm not around. From this day forward, the only kisses you'll get under the mistletoe will be from me. Anywhere you go, I go."

This man.

But she wasn't about to make it easy for him. "What if I wanted to teach in Antarctica?" she sassed.

He shrugged. "I'd buy thicker socks and follow you there."

"We're really doing this?" she asked, hope and anticipation coating her words.

A boyish half-grin graced his lips. "You wanted adventure, right?"

"Yeah."

"I can't think of anything more adventurous than following through on a mistletoe love match." He handed her his mobile. "Type our response. You know what I want. The decision is yours."

She reread the text.

Ralph Dagby: Merry Christmas! Louise and I hope you were touched by the magic of the season. We'd love to have you continue as volunteers at Helping Hands. Yes or no, will you be staying in Denver?

She studied the mistletoe, then returned her attention to Alec's mobile. Breathless with excitement, she typed three letters.

Y, E, S.

Send.

Holiday-infused delight washed over her. She handed the mobile to Alec, and her beautiful wanker smiled from ear to ear. "You look like a kid on Christmas," she said, tracing the outline of his grin.

"Under the circumstances, I should be smiling like a kid on Christmas."

"I get that it is officially Christmas, but you haven't gotten any gifts yet."

"That's not true." He gestured toward the darkened hearth. The fire had petered out, but the scent of the burnt Yule log lingered in the air.

What Christmas gift was in there?

"Is this about your Christmas Eve wish? Have you decided to tell me what you wished for?" she pressed.

Love and unyielding devotion shined in his eyes. "I don't have to tell you what I wished for."

"And why is that?" she asked, trying to read the man.

He glanced at the mobile, then held her gaze. "Because, Calliope Cress, the text you just sent made my Christmas Eve wish come true."

If you're swooning over Calliope and Alec, you're in luck. Our sassy Brit and slightly uptight doc-in-training are part of the Nanny Love Match books. Prepare to fall arse-over-elbow in love with your next favorite rom-com series. Visit www.Krista Sandor.com to learn more.

take a pic to
learn more

Also by Krista Sandor

The Nanny Love Match Series

A nanny/boss romantic comedy series

Book One: The Nanny and the Nerd

Book Two: The Nanny and the Hothead

Book Three: The Nanny and the Beefcake

Book Four: The Nanny and the Heartthrob

Love Match Legacy Books

The Nanny Love Match kids find their perfect match

The Sebastian Guarantee

The Oscar Escape

The Bergen Brothers Series

A steamy billionaire brothers romantic comedy series

Book One: Man Fast

Book Two: Man Feast

Book Three: Man Find

Bergen Brothers: The Complete Series+Bonus Short Story

The Farm to Mabel Duet

A brother's best friend romance set in a small-town

Book One: Farm to Mabel

Book Two: Horn of Plenty

Farm to Mabel: The Complete Duet

The Langley Park Series

A suspenseful, sexy second-chance at love series

Book One: The Road Home

Book Two: The Sound of Home

Book Three: The Beginning of Home

Book Four: The Measure of Home

Book Five: The Story of Home

Box Set (Books 1-5 + Bonus Scene)

Own the Eights Series

A delightfully sexy enemies-to-lovers series

Book One: Own the Eights

Book Two: Own the Eights Gets Married

Book Three: Own the Eights Maybe Baby

Box Set (Books 1-3)

STANDALONES

The Kiss Keeper

A toe-curlingly hot opposites attract romance

Not Your Average Vixen

An enemies-to-lovers super-steamy holiday romance

Sign up for Krista's newsletter to get all the up-to-date Krista Sandor Romance news!

Learn more at

www.KristaSandor.com

About the Author

If there's one thing Krista Sandor knows for sure, it's that romance saved her sanity. After she was diagnosed with Multiple Sclerosis in 2015, her world turned upside down. During those difficult first days, her dear friend sent her a romance novel. That kind gesture provided the escape she needed and ignited her love of the genre. Inspired by strong heroines and happily ever afters, Krista decided to write her own romance series. Today, she is an MS warrior, living life to the fullest. When she's not writing, you can find her running 5Ks with her husband and chasing after their growing boys in Denver, Colorado.

Never miss a release, contest, or author event! Visit www. KristaSandor.com to learn more.